THE GREEN-EYED QUEEN OF SUICIDE CITY

# THE GREEN-EYED QUEEN OF SUICIDE CITY

### A NOVEL

### Kevin Marc Fournier

GREAT PLAINS
TEEN FICTION

Copyright ©2012 Kevin Marc Fournier

Great Plains Teen Fiction
(an imprint of Great Plains Publications)
345-955 Portage Avenue
Winnipeg, MB R3G 0P9
www.greatplains.mb.ca

All rights reserved. No part of this publication may be reproduced or transmitted in any form or in any means, or stored in a database and retrieval system, without the prior written permission of Great Plains Publications, or, in the case of photocopying or other reprographic copying, a license from Access Copyright (Canadian Copyright Licensing Agency), 1 Yonge Street, Suite 1900, Toronto, Ontario, Canada, M5E 1E5.

Great Plains Publications gratefully acknowledges the financial support provided for its publishing program by the Government of Canada through the Canada Book Fund; the Canada Council for the Arts; the Province of Manitoba through the Book Publishing Tax Credit and the Book Publisher Marketing Assistance Program; and the Manitoba Arts Council.

Design & Typography by Relish Design Studio Inc.
Printed in Canada by Friesens

**LIBRARY AND ARCHIVES CANADA CATALOGUING IN PUBLICATION**

Fournier, Kevin Marc, 1974-
   Green-eyed queen of Suicide City / Kevin Marc Fournier.

Issued also in electronic formats.
ISBN 978-1-926531-26-7
   I. Title.

PS8611.O874G74 2012      jC813'.6      C2011-907036-7

ENVIRONMENTAL BENEFITS STATEMENT

Great Plains Publications saved the following resources by printing the pages of this book on chlorine free paper made with 100% post-consumer waste.

| TREES | WATER | ENERGY | SOLID WASTE | GREENHOUSE GASES |
|---|---|---|---|---|
| 6 FULLY GROWN | 2,654 GALLONS | 2 MILLION BTUs | 168 POUNDS | 588 POUNDS |

 Environmental impact estimates were made using the Environmental Paper Network Paper Calculator. For more information visit www.papercalculator.org

FSC
www.fsc.org
MIX
Paper from responsible sources
FSC® C016245

[I]n a certain faraway land the cold is so intense that words freeze as soon as they are uttered, and after some time then thaw and become audible, so that words spoken in winter go unheard until the next summer.—Plutarch, *Moralia*

A pregnant woman saw a baker carrying loaves on his bare shoulder. She was at once filled with such a craving for his flesh that she refused to taste any food till her husband persuaded the baker, by the offer of a large sum, to allow his wife to bite him. The man yielded, and the woman fleshed her teeth in his shoulder twice; but he held out no longer. The wife bore twins on three occasions, twice living, the third time dead.
— the Reverend S. Baring-Gould, *The Book of Werewolves*

*for Sarah,
who never fails to make me feel amazed,
amused, confounded, delighted & grateful*

# 1

IT WAS THE COLDEST WINTER I CAN REMEMBER EVER, MY MOTHER was eight months pregnant, and our friend Addy Mack came to stay with us for a couple weeks over the Christmas break. Addy and her mother had moved out to Montreal a year and a half before; it had been a year and a half since we'd seen her.

I had just turned fourteen in November. Addy and my brother Jack would be turning sixteen in a few weeks—they were born on the same day, just eleven hours apart, but I was always closer to Addy even though I was younger. I was the one who loved her most because I was the one who understood her best, and who missed her the most when she was always gone.

Winter had come abruptly. It had been pretty warm, right up until late October, then one morning it was cold when we left for school in the morning and it kept getting steadily colder all day long. The temperature dropped two degrees every hour and it never went up again. The river froze so quickly that people who lived along the banks could hear it turning into ice overnight; they said it sounded like something in pain.

It was around that time that Rose Lepine from Jack's class went missing, and they found her two weeks later, half buried under a snowbank in Beaconsfield Park. She had gone to bed like normal the night she disappeared, and must have slipped out the window, or snuck out the door after her parents passed out.

When they found her she was wearing nothing but her winter boots and a thin and summer sort of dress, probably the prettiest thing she owned. Her body was near some bushes, a few feet away from the trail, where the bank slopes down to the river.

She was lying on her side still half covered by the snow, looking sweet and peaceful and beautifully preserved, with her hands folded beneath her cheeks like she had just nestled down for a long winter's nap.

Of course most people said it must have been an accident, that she was probably drunk or high and just passed out. Some people said they heard she had snuck out to meet an older boy, or maybe it was even murder, but that was just making stuff up.

We all figured it was suicide. Maybe she *was* drunk or high, to help her over the hard part, but suicide all the same. You know her older sister Bethany had committed suicide a little more than a year before, and Rose had never really gotten over it. With Bethany, she was sixteen I think, it was the night before Halloween—something about that family and the holidays—and they found her in the closet of her bedroom, hanging by a man's tie. It was a black tie with red stripes, or a red tie with black stripes, and they couldn't figure out whose it was or where it came from. She'd taken almost a whole bottle of extra-strength Tylenol, so she might have died anyway even without the hanging. I'm not sure what she was wearing. They never found out about that tie, I do know that.

So this is why we figured that Rose the next year was suicide too, cause her older sister was pretty cool. And Jack says he remembers a conversation about the best way to die, a bunch of them all talking, and everyone agreed they'd heard freezing to death was supposed to be the sweetest, once you got to the part where you go all numb. Their parents moved away soon after Rose's body was found. Because let's face it, if one of your daughters commits suicide, everyone feels sorry for you, but if both your kids off themselves, it starts to look like you're pretty useless.

Anyway, we had picked Addy up at the airport the very first day of the holidays, that Friday night. Her plane got in pretty late, something like ten-thirty or eleven. She came down the escalator wearing a thin black jacket and an Expos cap, carrying a backpack crammed with clothes and a couple small presents, and nothing else. No other luggage, no mitts, no winter gear.

Addy hadn't grown any taller at all since she'd moved away and I had, so that now we were the same height, and that made it seem to me as if she had shrunk, somehow. And then of course there was her hair, her beautiful red-brown hair, which I was so used to seeing drop halfway down her back all dark and thick, or falling forward to hide her face, or winding itself lovingly around her throat as she slept. Her beautiful hair had been all chopped off; it barely came down to her ears.

But other than that she was just the same Addy as ever, with the same big green eyes, the same round and freckled cat's face. Her eyes are actually two different colours, though a lot of people don't notice it right away unless they're really looking, because her left eye is that kind of hazel colour that people call green even though it really isn't, but her right eye is green for real, green as a blade of grass.

The first thing she said, before she even said hello, as soon as she caught sight of me she called out, "Hey, Natalie! How's your mom? Did she have a baby yet?"

"No," I said. I had spoken to her on the phone just the night before, and she'd asked me the same thing then.

"Good," she said, nodding her head approvingly and narrowing her eyes. The due date wasn't until the second week of January—just four days after Jack and Addy's birthday, actually—but I knew she was really hoping the baby would come early, while she was here. She was pretty confident that it would.

"The third one's always early," she'd told me. "I looked it up. Anyway, they'll do it for *me*."

I don't know who she thought "they" were. Mom and Davey, maybe? The doctors? I didn't ask.

Davey made her put on his parka before he'd let us leave the airport, she said she didn't need it but he told her we weren't going anywhere with her dressed like that, and what the hell was she thinking? He had two heavy sweaters underneath the parka, and his scarf and gloves and toque of course, but he still complained the whole way home. He hates the cold and the cold hates him.

Addy complained the whole way too, because it was so cold that as soon as she stepped outside and we started to make our way to the parking lot, a blast of icy wind whipped her across the face and spun her around, and it was so cold her nose started to bleed. Addy always did get nosebleeds really easily, as long as I can remember—if she sneezed too hard or rubbed her nose, if the air was too dry or too humid, if it was too hot or too cold. Or when she was sleeping, if she had a particularly exciting nightmare, and then she might wake up with the side of her face and a bunch of her hair all stuck to the pillow with a crust of dried blood.

Sometimes she wouldn't even realize it was bleeding, and she'd go happily along, doing whatever she was doing, and leaving a little trail of bright red splats in her path. I often thought that if she were Hansel and Gretel in that story, she wouldn't need to leave a trail of stones or bread crumbs behind her, she could just give her nose a good rub and then follow the drops of blood back home. Only, Addy being Addy, she probably wouldn't bother. She'd probably be happier getting lost in the woods anyway.

"Holy crap," she said as we piled into the car. "I don't remember it being *this* bad. What did you guys do to this place?" As if she'd left the city and its climate in our particular care when she'd moved away, and we'd really let it go to hell. Davey started going on about how she'd better not get blood on his good parka, but no one had any Kleenex or anything, so I had to give her one of my mittens to hold over her nose, and she complained about that too: "Ah, *man*," she said, "it smells like wet cat ass. Where have you been sticking this thing?"

When we arrived at our house the first thing she did was make a beeline for my mother—shedding her hat, Davey's parka, and my bloody mitten in a trail across the kitchen floor—and asked to feel her belly.

Mom was in the armchair in the living room, nearly immobile under a mountain of blankets, sipping hot fruity tea and reading a fashion mag. She made a face when she noticed Addy's nose, but didn't say anything. Jack's fat cat, Typhus, was lying on the floor, curled on top of her feet and keeping them warm. He raised his head and hissed wickedly at Addy as she came towards them. He'd gotten stupid protective of Mom since she was pregnant, and Mom had to push him up with one foot and then give him a kick in the ribs with the other to make him go away.

When I was younger, sometimes it depressed me to think that I was never going to turn out as beautiful as my mother. Not that she's ever got all that much happiness or advantage out of being so beautiful, I guess, except that she probably makes more tips that way, working as a waitress. But she's tall and lovely and lean, and she's got that long honey-coloured hair and pale, perfect, white and pink skin, and those light blue eyes the shape of almonds. She has dimples when she smiles, and when she frowns—which let's face it, is considerably more often—her eyes will crinkle at the edges and her mouth pouts up in a pretty adorable way.

Jack looks much more like our mom than I do. He's tall like her, even at fourteen or fifteen he was tall as her already, and he smiles the same smile and when he frowns his mouth makes the same pout. But the biggest thing is the eyes. He has our mom's eyes exactly, but his hair and his skin are dark like our father's, so that those pale blue eyes in his lean brown face look absolutely startling, almost unreal, when he bothers to open them all the way. By the time we were in our teens, every girl I knew in school was half in love with him.

I take more after our father. I had never really met him, he left before I was born, but I have a few old photographs, and I can definitely see myself in him: shorter and a bit thicker than Mom, with brown eyes and olive skin, thick black difficult hair and a completely boring face, except for a nose that's just a little bit bigger than anybody's nose needs to be. Just like me.

Mom nagged at Addy for not taking off her shoes when she came into the house, sat awkwardly up to give her a hug, and then—with a great deal of complaining that was only about one-quarter sincere—lifted her sweater and guided Addy's hand over her firm, fat stomach until she could feel the baby move.

"You know what would be cool?" said Addy. "If we got snowed into the house and couldn't get out, and you went into labour, and we had to deliver the baby ourselves."

"Or you know what would be even cooler?" said Mom. "If that *didn't* happen and I have the baby safely in the hospital, with nurses and doctors and lots of nice drugs."

"That's okay," said Addy comfortingly, "I've been reading up, so if it does happen, you don't need to worry. I'm ready."

Addy shared my room whenever she came to stay with us, on the first floor, in the back by the kitchen. Jack's room was on the second floor, across the hall from Mom and Davey's room, which was going to suck for him when the baby came and cried all night. When they first got pregnant, Mom and Davey had talked about how we'd have to move, find a bigger place to live. After a while they stopped talking about that, and started talking about fixing up the basement instead. Get the landlord to go halfers with them on it, or maybe he'd pay for the materials if Jack and Davey did all the labour. Put down some carpet over the concrete and panel over the insulation on the walls and make a bedroom for Jack down there, and then the new baby could have his old room across the hall. But that wasn't going to happen until at least the spring if it ever happened at all.

Jack and I used to argue about whose room was smaller, his or mine. If you only measured along the floor, his was bigger by a couple feet each way, but he said it didn't count because the ceiling in his room sloped so much and you couldn't even stand upright in the whole back half of his room, which I said *that* didn't count because the back half of his room was where his bed was, so he wasn't going to be standing up there anyway.

I had the bunk bed in my room, the same bunk bed Jack and I used to share when we were just little and living in that apartment on Pritchard Ave, and that's where Addy slept whenever she stayed with us, up on the top bunk above me.

"It's freezing in here," she complained as we changed into our pajamas. "Is that window even closed? Hey, Nat, show me your toes."

I'd gotten my first ever pedicure in the fall, but that was four months before, almost all of the nail polish had chipped and faded away by then. I showed her anyway. "Isn't it cold in Montreal?" I said. "I thought you told me it was worse because it's a wet cold."
"Yeah, well, I lied, this is way worse. I like that colour, that's a good colour on you, you should get 'em painted again. Good thing you can't chew your toenails, eh?"
"I wish I could go back to Montreal with you," I said. "It's not like there's going to be room for me anyway when the baby comes," I joked, though it probably wasn't only a joke. Not totally a joke.
"We could always swap places," she said. "Like when it's time to go back to the airport, we'll wrap ourselves up in scarves and stuff for the cold so they can't see our faces, and then we'll go to the bathroom right before boarding and switch clothes—"
"Oh, come on, we wouldn't fool anyone for a second. And why would we have scarves over our faces inside the airport, anyway?"
She shrugged. "Well, the plan probably does need a little polishing, but I bet we could pull it off somehow. We've got a couple weeks to think of something. Anyway, you're the one who wants to switch places, I don't know why. I'm just trying to help you out here. I mean Montreal's nice but it's not *that* nice. Do you really want to have to live with my mom?"
As she swung herself up the ladder to the top bunk, she told me that she had finally stopped having her nightmares, she'd figured out how to get rid of them.
"How?" I asked her.
"It's easy," she said. "I just don't sleep anymore. You can't have nightmares," she pointed out reasonably, "if you're always awake. I can't believe it took me so long to think of it. Don't worry, though, I won't keep you up. I like just lying there quietly in the dark, you get a lot of thinking done."
I was accustomed to believing that Addy was capable of just about anything, but this sounded pretty unlikely even to me. "How long do you think you can keep that up?" I asked her.

"I don't know," she said. "Couple months so far. It's not so bad. You hallucinate a little bit, but that's pretty cool, too."

"Don't you need sleep to survive?"

"Not yet," she said cheerfully. "Are these all the blankets you got?"

"Sorry," I said, "Mom's been hoarding all the extra blankets in the house. She says she's freezing for two now."

"That doesn't make any sense," Addy complained. "She's like a walrus with all that blubber, she shouldn't need any blankets at all."

"Yeah, well, you can tell her that, I'm not gonna."

The next morning, I woke up to the wind wailing through the walls and pelting ice against my window. The clock said 6:36. Instead of sticking my head into the pillow and trying to get back to sleep, I lay there and listened a minute. All I could hear was winter. I slipped out of the bottom bunk as quietly as I could and climbed halfway up the ladder, but Addy was already gone, blankets thrown back, sheets and pillow cool to the touch. It had snowed all night and was snowing still, just like Addy had asked it to. In Beaconsfield Park, the snow must have been swirling through the dark and covering over Rose's frozen body, but of course I had no idea at the time.

# 2

ROSE ONCE WROTE A STORY FOR HER GRADE TEN ENGLISH CLASS about an old homeless woman who died in a blizzard one winter's night, and was completely covered over with snow. Everyone thought she was only a normal snowman; the children put an old hat and scarf on her, gave her eyes and a nose of gravel, and played around her all winter. When spring came and the snow melted, the old woman melted with it, soaking into the ground, and blue and yellow flowers grew where once she stood. Her English teacher gave her a C. "Too short. Ending doesn't make sense," he wrote in red ink at the bottom of the page.

She thought of that story the night she died, as the snow piled and swept over her shivering body. Her father had often told them about the time he almost froze to death, on a hunting trip up north, and how he'd realized how close he was to dying when he suddenly felt perfectly warm, peaceful and sleepy. That was how Rose had imagined it would be for her: warm, peaceful, and just like drifting sweetly off to sleep. She kept waiting for that to come; she kept telling herself that it would come. Instead it was cold and biting and painful, right up until the bitter end. She remembered the story, and what the teacher wrote at the bottom. Her last coherent thought before she died was that they ought to write those words on her gravestone: "Her life was too short, and the ending didn't make sense."

The next thing Rose knew, she was in a small and empty room where the light leaked dimly in through a dirty window. She was lying on the bare, wood floor, and chilled to the bone, shivering uncontrollably. She didn't know where she was or why, but she knew that she had died, and this was death.

Her ears and fingers were swollen, stiff and biting with pain; her toes burned and itched as if insects had burrowed into them. The skin on her face was drawn unbearably tight, her nose was running and her eyes were stinging and wet. She was hungry, too, so hungry her stomach was cramping with pain. The memory of her last supper and how she'd barely picked at the food on her plate, too excited to eat, came back to her with excruciating clarity.

The room was dingy, airless, and not much larger than a closet. There was no light to turn on and no door to open, nothing but that single window, the cracked glass too grimy to see through. She tried to push it open but it was stuck, and her fingers, frozen, were clumsy and stiff, making it difficult to get a grip. If the window wouldn't open, Rose was prepared to start punching the glass where it was cracked and keep punching until she smashed through, even if it smashed and slashed her hand to a pulp in the process. *What does it matter*, she thought, *I'm dead already*. The idea was almost appealing, but with one last push it finally moved—only an inch, but enough for her to get her hands under the frame and work it slowly open.

She found herself looking out on a deserted city street from the second floor of a squat, beige and ugly apartment block. Judging by the half-light, it was mid-evening or very early morning, gloomy under a mud-coloured sky. There were no people in sight, no cars, no sound or sign of life. All she could see, on both sides of the street and stretching in either direction, were rows and rows of buildings, all exactly the same as the one she was in.

There was no snow on the ground; it wasn't the middle of winter here. There were weeds pushing through the cracks in the pavement, green leaves on the trees. The trees themselves grew not in an ordinary, orderly row along the boulevard, but right out in the middle of the street, straight up through the asphalt: gnarled and dwarfish trees with thick, scabrous bark and sparse leaves so darkly green they looked almost black.

As she leaned out and looked down, the wind cold and dry across her face, she could hear sounds in the distance, directionless, carried and distorted by the swirling wind—footsteps, something scraping, a voice or something like a voice, shrill and indistinct—but still she could see no one. Rose didn't know whether to scream, or cry, or laugh. She couldn't understand where she was, or why, whether this was some kind of special punishment for her or merely death for everybody. She wondered if she was alone here, and almost hoped it was so. But she had hated the city when she was alive; to be stuck in one forever, dead, seemed cruelly unfair. She felt an overwhelming urge to escape, to get free of this little room and away from these streets forever.

There was no way out of the room but the window, and there was no way down from the window but to jump. She had begun to lift one leg over the sill when she heard a voice call out, "I wouldn't do that if I were you."

It was a man in the middle of the street below, standing next to a tree no taller than he was. He seemed to have appeared out of nowhere, Rose could have sworn there'd been no one there a moment ago. He was a small, bony man with short yellow hair, livid freckles and long, thin lips, looking up at the window with his head tilted to one side. A grubby white sack lay on the ground at his feet.

"Why not?" she called back. "What, am I gonna die again?"

"No," he said gently. "But you'll wish you could. You'll hurt, even more than you already do. Forever."

She almost laughed; she could hardly imagine being in more pain than she already was. But there was something in his voice, and in his face as he looked up at her, that made her take him seriously; something soft, calm, and infinitely sad. He walked a few feet closer to the building, hands in the pockets of his ragged pants. "I can't talk you into staying up there, can I?"

"No, you can't," she said. "I'm cold, I'm hungry. I'm coming down."

"You'll be just as cold and hungry down here. Up there at least you're safe." But he shook his head knowingly, like someone who has had this same conversation before and knows how it will end anyway. "How did you do it?" he asked her.

"I don't know," she said. "I just woke up here. There's no door, there's no way out, nothing."

"Did you hang yourself?" he asked, making a pulling gesture at his neck. "No? You should always hang yourself," he said. "Then you're still dead, but at least you have the rope. Well, tell me what you're wearing, then."

She looked up and down the street again, but there was no other person in sight.

"Clothes," he said patiently. "If you promise to give me a piece of your clothing, I'll help you get down without hurting yourself."

"All I have is my dress," she said. "I'm not giving you my dress."

A spasm of irritation passed across his face. "You must have something else. Tights, stockings, socks? Shoes? How long is your dress then, does it go down past your knees?"

She nodded, warily, willing to humour him for the moment. What mattered now was getting down; once she was down on the street she could run, fight, do whatever she had to do. She just had to humour him until he helped her down.

"Fine," he said. "I'll cut a strip off the bottom of your dress, that will have to do. Is it a deal?" He didn't wait for an answer, he turned away and walked back to the tree, choosing a short thick branch and breaking it off. It snapped off easily, with a hollow crack like dead wood, but the tree gave out a scream, a high-pitched shriek of pain that made Rose wince to hear it, piercing her ears, and a dark liquid, like black-red blood, spurted from the wound. He moved his bundle out of the way of the pooling liquid, off to the side so it wouldn't get wet. The leaves on the broken branch dried up, shrivelled, and fell off like a time-lapse film of autumn, and the wind snatched them away.

"Back away from the window," he said. "All the way back, I don't want to hit you."

The tree was still screaming, still pulsing out blood onto the street. It was the most hideous sound that Rose had ever heard. "When will it stop?" she asked.

"It won't," he said. "Not ever. Now back away from the window."

It took him several attempts, the stick clattering harmlessly against the side of the building and falling back to the sidewalk, before he finally got it to sail through the open window and into the room, where it skittered across the floor. Rose picked it up gingerly, touching the broken end with the tip of her finger: and her fingertip came away all sticky and red.

"Break all the glass out of the window," he told her. "Get it all out of there. But be careful. If you cut yourself, you'll bleed forever; if you hurt yourself, you'll hurt forever. That's the way it works from now on—nothing ever gets better, you never heal, you never even get used to the pain. Everything always only gets worse. Do you believe me?"

She nodded. "I believe you."

"Good," he said, that note of gentleness returning to his voice. "You'd better. Now take your time. Time's one thing you'll always have no end of any more."

He went back across the street to his bundle, kneeling down and untying the knot at the top. It spilled open to reveal great heaps of rags and clothing. He pulled out a string of them, shirts and rags all wound and twisted and tied together to make a long ungainly rope. He drew it out from the pile and coiled it around his arm slowly and patiently, untangling it as he went, testing every knot.

And Rose held the stick with both hands, and swung it at the crack in the glass as hard as if it were somebody's face, and the glass shattered and burst from the frame, raining down on the street below.

The man used a rag to brush the shards of glass carefully away from the pavement beneath the window before setting down his makeshift rope. One end of this rope had a rock in it, tied inside a shirtsleeve. Telling Rose again to step back, he threw it up through the open window, taking several tries again. "Loop it through the window frame and feed it back down to me," he told her.

The clothes and rags were disgusting, so caked with dirt and soaked through with blood they were spongy to the touch and smelled like rotting meat. She dry-heaved as she handled it and would have vomited for sure if there were anything in her stomach. When she finished feeding it through the window frame and he had both ends of the rope at the bottom, he began twisting the two strands tightly together.

"Use the stick to prop the window open," he told her. "You don't want it falling when you're halfway down. That's it, test it, make sure it'll hold. Take your time coming down."

Though the man below showed no sign of feeling cold at all, Rose was still frozen right through, and her fingers felt numb and clumsy as she climbed onto the ledge and wrapped herself around the rope. She turned around, planting her boots against the side of the building as her body swung free of the ledge. She had to hold her face awkwardly away from the rancid clothing, and the acrid smell stung her eyes and made her gag. She worked her way down with agonizing slowness, step by cautious step, and with the man's warnings running through her mind she refused to look down, afraid of becoming dizzy. It came as a shock when she suddenly felt a hand touch her shoulder lightly, and she almost lost her grip.

"You can let go now," the man said. "You made it."

She looked down. The pavement was right below her. She needed only to lower her legs to be standing.

"You lied to me," he said pleasantly. "You've got boots and all, now don't you?" She backed a few cautious steps away from him, as he looked her over.

"You're just a child," he said. It sounded like a complaint. "I'm Malcolm," he said, and extended a hand to shake hers. She ignored it, and backed away a little further.

"You've done this before," she said. "Helped people down."

"It's something to do." He shrugged. "Better than thinking, anyway. I was pretty useless to other people when I was alive, I might as well make use of myself now I'm here."

"How long have you... been here?"

"I don't know," he said. "To be honest with you, I don't want to know any more." He began untwisting the rope and drawing it carefully back through the window frame. "It was 1947 when I slit my wrists. You can do the math yourself, if you like."

Looking at him again, Rose realized that he wasn't wearing a long-sleeved shirt, as she'd thought from a distance. His sleeves came down just past his elbows, but his forearms and wrists were bound round with tight black rags. His pants were ragged and torn and his feet were bare, the toes spatulate and blistered, the nails yellow and cracked.

"Are we in hell?" she asked him.

"We're dead," he said. "It's what you wanted, isn't it? It's what we all thought we wanted."

Down here on the street, the wind was blowing even stronger, whipping her fine brown hair around her face. Strange noises travelled on the wind, metallic moans and distorted cries of pain and breaking, while the tree behind her continued to pulse blood and shriek incessantly. The sound was unbearable.

Rose wondered if she would be able to outrun the man. She had always been a strong runner when she was alive, but her whole body felt so stiff and frigid, she wasn't sure how fast she'd be able to make her legs move. Still, this might be her best and perhaps her only chance to get away from him, now while he was so focused on his rope. She turned abruptly, and darted away as hard as she could. The wind pushed back at her, but a kind of bursting fear impelled her, and she didn't look behind to see if he was following, she just ran.

When she had looked up and down the street from the window, it had stretched on straight and unbroken in both directions for as far as the eye could see, but now it seemed as if she had hardly run a hundred yards when a building loomed up directly in front of her, and she found herself at an intersection. Startled, she came to a stop in the middle of the street.

Directly in front of her was a building in the shape of a church, but painted the colour of cotton candy, a weak, appalling pink. She could see only a single window in the whole building, wide and round and set high above the entranceway. Seven wide stone steps lead up to a pair of broad oak doors.

Down the street to her left she could see rows of townhouses, shabby, rundown and cheaply made, all busted windows and bubbling, flaking stucco. None of the houses had windows on the ground floor, and the trees down that street were a little taller and closer together. The wind had shifted around again, as if it wanted to push her in that direction. Along the street to her right, the houses looked newer, larger, and less rundown, and the trees were smaller and further apart, but the wind was coming from that way, carrying with it intolerable sounds and smells.

At an impulse she ran straight ahead, up the steps and to the doors of the church. She grabbed the doorknobs but neither of them would turn, she pushed and pulled but the doors wouldn't budge. Looking closer, she realized that there were no hinges on the doors and not even the slightest gap between them, nor any gap between the wood of the doors and the building around them. They weren't real doors at all, just made to look that way. There was no opening: no way inside.

Rose turned around. Malcolm was right behind her, standing at the bottom of the steps. He dropped his bundle to the ground. It was untied, and some of the rags and strips of cloth spilled out onto the sidewalk, but he took no notice. He kept his eyes on her.

Reaching into the back pocket of his jeans, Malcolm pulled out a small yellow rag that had been folded into a tidy rectangle. He placed this in the palm of his hand and carefully unfolded it as he climbed the steps towards her. Inside the rag was a straight razor with a cracked black and plastic handle. The blade, as he opened it, showed itself pitted red and brown with blood and rust.

"I was naked when I got here, myself," he said. "Nice glass of wine, a warm bath, and put an end to it, you know? That was the idea. So all I had when I woke up was this." He waved the blade in front of his face.

He was standing uncomfortably close to her now, just one step below her. She briefly considered trying to push him down the stairs and then running away again, but it seemed hopeless. Even if she got past him without getting slashed, where was she going to go?

"What's your name?" Malcolm asked. "Rose? A deal's a deal, Rose. Hold still, now, I wouldn't want to nick you." Going down on one knee, he pulled the hem of her dress towards him and pushed the edge of the razor through the material, just above her knees. The blade was dull with age and use, more tearing the fabric than cutting, but it did the job.

"Those are good-looking boots," he commented as he worked. "You're lucky to have them, but I'd be careful if I were you. Turn around a little... that's right. Boots like that, a lot of people here are going to want to take them from you. Shoes of any kind are a pretty valuable commodity around here. Not so many people kill themselves with their shoes on—it's not something you think you're going to need. Turn a little more, now."

Working steadily and confidently, he cut and tore a two-and-a-half-inch wide strip off the bottom of her dress. It fell to the ground in a ring around her feet, and she stepped out and away from it, backing up against the doors that weren't really doors.

Standing, Malcolm took the yellow rag and carefully, almost lovingly wrapped his razor up again, replacing it in his pocket. He then took the strip of fabric he had cut for himself and descended the steps.

He added the piece of her dress to his bundle, and began gathering up the rags that had spilled out onto the pavement. Rose, coming down the steps after him, noticed a black and red striped necktie among them.

"Wait," she said when he picked up the tie to put it away. "Wait. That tie... can I see it?" She found she was shaking, slightly.

He gave her a long, quizzical look, then stepped towards her with a shrug, holding the necktie out. She took it and she held it and she looked down towards it, rubbing the material gently between her thumb and finger, but she wasn't really looking at it. She realized that she had no way of knowing if it really was the same one—the same tie that Bethany used to hang herself—though it looked like it could be. It looked just the same as she remembered it. She remembered it with utter clarity, too, as if she'd last seen it only yesterday. She felt that Malcolm was watching her face intently, searchingly, and she lifted her eyes to meet his.

"My sister," she explained. "My sister hanged herself with a tie like this. It was just like this one."

There passed across his kindly, ugly face an expression that could have been envy, just for a moment, and then it was gone, the gentle weary sadness returning to his eyes.

"Did she now?" he said lightly. "Hanged herself with a tie like that tie? And how long ago was that, then?"

"A year ago. A year and two months. She looked like me. She looked like I do now, but a little taller, and much prettier." Tears were slipping down her cheeks and into her mouth, but she didn't bother to try and fight them back. "Her name was Bethany."

Malcolm reached out to take the tie away from her, but Rose wasn't going to let it go. They stood there now, each holding one end of it.

"If she killed herself, she's here," he said. "She's here somewhere. That's what you want to know, isn't it?"

# 3

ROSE HAD STARTED HIGH SCHOOL THAT YEAR. HIGH SCHOOL and a new school. Rose, Jack, Conrad and that whole gang, they'd all moved on. I still had to do one more year of junior high, so that sucked for me. I'd always had my big brother in school with me before, and I'd always hung out more with him and Addy and Conrad and the rest of their friends than with any of the kids in my own grade.

So I got into the habit of walking with Jack to the high school in the mornings and hanging out with everyone for ten or fifteen minutes before walking back to my school, where I was usually pretty late for my first class. Also, sometimes I would cut out early at the end of the day if I thought I could get away with it, and head back to the high school to hang out in the afternoon, instead of just going straight home.

I remember seeing Rose there only once or twice. The first time I saw her it was a total shock for me. She had changed so much over the summer—gotten taller and skinnier so that now she looked just like her sister had. For a minute I thought I was seeing a ghost.

When I got closer, I saw that her face was still a bit rounder than her sister's had been, and she was still a bit shorter, not so lanky. But she'd been growing her hair out and had it in a braid like Bethany used to wear, and I'm certain that she was wearing some of her sister's old clothes, I recognized that outfit in particular from one of the pictures of Bethany that her family used to have on the fridge. Of course I didn't say anything. Probably she was just wearing her sister's old clothes to save money, but I don't know, it did seem a touch creepy. They looked good on her, though, Bethany always did have pretty good taste in clothes.

We chatted for a couple minutes, I told her about my mom being pregnant and puking all over the place all the time, and she told me she had heard, but she didn't seem very interested. That was okay. I thought she seemed happy, actually; she seemed more confident, not so shy and uncertain as I was used to her being. Anyway, we talked in a nothing sort of way for a couple minutes, and then the bell rang for classes to begin. She headed into the school and I had to run. We said see you later, and that was it. She dropped more or less out of my mind as I'm sure I dropped out of hers, and we didn't talk again between then and when she disappeared.

Of course I had known Rose for years, ever since her family had moved into the neighbourhood, when she and Jack and Addy were all in grade four together. She was almost pretty but not really pretty. She did well in school, but not too well. She usually seemed happy, but not too happy. She dressed the same as everyone else dressed, ate what everyone else ate, didn't hang out after school, went straight home, wasn't really out and around on the weekends.

You knew that money must be tight with her family, but that was pretty much true of everyone in our school. Really, the only thing that stood out about her, until her sister died, was that her family was from up north—I mean way, *way* up north, Nunavut up north—and you could get her to talk about how much she missed it.

In Nunavut, she told me, everyone keeps a kettle full of water on low boil on the stove, even when they're out, and when you drop by to visit someone you just let yourself in. If no one's home you make yourself a cup of tea off the kettle, and settle down to wait. In Nunavut they had a big grey dog named Todd, and when you look north you can see the curve of the earth. In the summer you have to put tinfoil over the windows to keep out the sun at night, and up in Iqaluit there's a street called the Road to Nowhere, she showed me a photo of her standing beside the street sign smiling and that's really what it says.

Now, Bethany was different. She was always the prettiest, coolest girl in school, everybody said so. She was the sort of girl who everybody wants to be friends with, at least partly because she never seemed to care whether anyone wanted to be her friend or not. She was always nice to you when she noticed you, but then she hardly ever noticed you, and you didn't blame her for *not* noticing you either, it was only natural, she had so much going on. God only knows why she'd want to kill herself. I never heard that she did a lot of drugs or anything like that, but maybe she did. Maybe she was sick, or I remember someone told me they heard that she was pregnant, but I'm pretty sure that was just bullshit, cause how would *they* know? Maybe there was no real reason at all, or a whole bunch of little reasons that all added up inside her mind. Maybe she was just tired. I get tired, sometimes.

No one's sure, the night she died, what time of night she died. It was Gate Night and a Friday night, and Rose and her parents all thought she had gone out to a party. There were a few she'd been invited to. Maybe the parties were an excuse and she went out somewhere else, somewhere secret. Or maybe she never left her room at all.

A month or two after she died, a rumour started going around that she *was* seen at those parties, all three of them at almost exactly midnight. In all three cases one or two people caught sight of her sitting in the corner, or standing off to the side in the kitchen, something like that, wearing a T-shirt, jeans and a red and black man's tie around her neck, just sitting or standing there, no drink in her hand and a sad blank expression on her face. Only, when the person tried to go over to her or say something to her, she disappeared. And so, of course, almost midnight must have been the moment she died, and this was her ghost saying goodbye.

This story made the rounds for quite a while, with more and more people claiming to be one of the ones who saw her, but I couldn't bring myself to believe in it, though I thought it was a lovely lie to tell. If I died suddenly and unexpectedly, how many people would miss me saying goodbye to them so much they'd pretend they saw my ghost?

There was a lot of talk about the fact that her parents didn't even find her body; it hanged there in the closet, unnoticed, for twenty-four hours or more. But that seemed unfair to me—it's not like Bethany left a note, or like they weren't concerned. They just figured she'd gone out and hadn't come home, that she had crashed at one of the parties or a friend's place. They called around to some of her friends, the ones they had phone numbers for, and when no one could say they had seen her or knew where she might be, they started to get really worried, they even called the police to file a missing persons report. But why should they have looked in her closet? The door was closed and everything appeared normal. So it was Rose who found her hanging.

The police had come. This was quite late. Rose said it was after eleven when they showed up—probably they were pretty busy with it being Halloween night and everything. Anyway, they were looking through pictures of her, asking questions and taking down lots of details, and one of them asked Rose if she would go through her sister's room and make note of anything and everything that she thought might be missing, cause if she'd run away on purpose, planned it, she probably would have taken a few changes of clothes and some personal things, and I guess they figured that Rose would be more likely to know what Bethany owned or didn't own than her parents would. So Rose was the one who opened the closet door and found Bethany's body hanging there.

We all went to the funeral. It was the first funeral I had ever been to. The church made a great impression on me. I had only been inside a church once before, back when I was six and I was the flower girl at my Aunt Tracy's wedding, but this was very different. This one was much more impressive, so dark, and all the stained-glass windows, the polished uncomfortable pews, and all the pictures and plaster statuettes along the walls depicting Jesus, mostly showing him being tortured or dying. I desperately wished I could walk around and get a better look at them, they were all so ugly and sincere.

But the funeral itself was disappointing. There was a casket up front with flowers on it, but the lid was closed and we never got to look. There wasn't as much crying as I expected, except out of some poor baby sitting somewhere up near the front, and its mother had to get up and go stand in the back, making shushing noises that sounded more angry than soothing, pacing back and forth and jostling the poor thing up and down until it spat up all over the front of her dress, and served her right.

It was cold in there when we first arrived, and then by the end it was stifling hot and stuffy, the place was so crowded. The ceremony seemed to drag on forever, like a punishment, and all of the people who got up to talk about Bethany, they mostly talked about how smart she was and what good grades she got and how proud she made her parents and how much she loved her little sister, which none of that sounded like Bethany to me, but then I never really knew her all that well. And of course they all talked about how beautiful she was, which was true, but really it was like they could have been talking about just any made-up girl in the world instead of Bethany in particular.

But what really shocked me was that no one mentioned or even, as I thought, alluded to the way she died at all. I remember one person said that Bethany had an "illness" that took her life—meaning, of course, that she must have had some kind of mental illness that made her commit suicide—but I didn't pick up on that right away. I thought it was an outright lie. I guess it would have been more shocking if they *had* talked about it openly, but I thought that a funeral was something official, almost a sort of legal ceremony like a wedding is.

The Saturday after Bethany's funeral it was my thirteenth birthday party. Mom had said I could invite eleven people, and then there would be thirteen including Jack and me, one for each of my years, but I handed out more like seventeen or eighteen invitations because I figured only half of the people I invited would actually come. I gave them out the week before Halloween, so that's why Rose got one too. Of course I never expected her to show up after Bethany's death and everything, but she did.

She arrived about an hour and a half after everyone else. Her cheeks and nose were bright red even though it wasn't that cold a night, and she was carrying a big box wrapped in green and silver paper.

No one else had brought a present. The invitations all said not to. Mom insisted on that. So I didn't want to open the gift in front of everybody else, but I also didn't want to make Rose feel bad for bringing it either, so I took her to my bedroom—I think I said something about showing her around, since she'd never been to our house before—and I opened it there.

It was a whole outfit: leggings, skirt, matching shirt. I saw the tag and it didn't come from a super expensive store but not a cheap one, either. I think I said Jesus Christ or something, because now I'd have to buy her a Christmas gift in return, and where was I gonna come up with that kind of money? Then Rose looked so awkward and unhappy as I laid out the clothes on my bed that I had to give her a hug, and I gave her a quick kiss on her cold cheek and told her I loved it, that it was super cute, which was true. I put the outfit on right then and wore it for the rest of the party. It fit perfectly.

Rose was the sixteenth person to arrive. I was counting them cause I knew that Mom was going to give me hell for inviting too many guests. She wouldn't say anything in front of everybody, but I'd get it the next day. After serving the first round of food and drinks and making sure everyone was settled, Mom and Davey had gone up to their bedroom to watch TV and stay out of the way. Every twenty minutes or so one of them would slip downstairs to get something from the kitchen and discreetly check that no one was drinking Davey's beer or making out in my bedroom or anything. Most of the food was gone by the time Rose arrived, she said she wasn't hungry but I made her a pot of tea because she didn't seem to be warming up at all. She must have been outside a long time.

She admitted to me later that she hadn't really wanted to come. Not because of me or she didn't think it would be fun, she just wasn't in a party kind of mood, which of course I could totally understand. But her parents had really pushed her to go. I guess after Bethany died, they felt they needed to make an effort and meddle in their other daughter's life—for a little while, anyway. They said it was important that she should go out, have a good time and take her mind off stuff, make some more friends. They bought the gift and made her take it.

So when she left her apartment to walk over—it was only a few blocks from our house, maybe a five-minute walk—she just walked up and down the dark streets for a long time, and in Beaconsfield Park along the river, thinking to herself.

There's that path that runs behind the monument to where the old Children's Hospital used to be, the one that someone spray-painted "the Devil's Walk" near the opening. I don't know why, I've never seen the Devil there, though I did once see an overcoat hanging from a high tree branch that when I first caught sight of it out of the corner of my eye, I could have sworn it was a whole body hanging there. It looked really spooky. You can follow the walk all the way along the river to St John's Park and the old cemetery, and she wandered along there a long time, it was a beautiful night with the stars all out and the river still mostly open, flowing slowly.

She told me she probably would have just walked around like that the whole evening and then gone home and lied to her parents, say she'd gone to the party and had a good time, if it wasn't for the present they'd made her take for me.

She couldn't take it back home with her, and she was tired of carrying it around. She didn't feel right just ditching it somewhere or throwing it in the garbage. She thought about leaving it on our doorstep but then she'd have to make some kind of embarrassing explanation on Monday, and what if someone caught sight of her through the window? It's actually kind of a miracle that in all that time, walking around in our neighbourhood alone on a Saturday night, no one just knocked her down and stole it from her, and maybe raped her around a bit.

So after about an hour of trying to figure out what to do with the stupid present, she said she suddenly started laughing at herself, because why the hell shouldn't she just go to the party and give it to me? It was far and away the simplest thing to do. Besides, she didn't have gloves on and she was getting pretty cold. But the funny part was that once she made up her mind to go and started heading to our house, she actually got kind of disoriented and had a hard time finding our street.

If you've never been to our neighbourhood, Point Douglas is kind of a little peninsula inside a bend of the river, and railway yards on the other side. There are lots of little streets that run in weird angles off each other and stop in dead ends or don't join up where you think they will. Lots of people get lost when they're new to the neighbourhood, but of course Rose had lived here for years, she should have known it as well as I did. Her brain must have gotten a little bit frozen. She said it was crazy, it was like the streets were shifting position even as she was walking along them, and she went in circles for what felt like half an hour, almost ready to cry, before Prince Edward Street suddenly popped up in front of her, and there was our house.

The weekend after my birthday, Rose invited me to her place for a sleepover. It was a Friday night, her parents were going out for the evening and they wanted Rose to have a friend over to keep her company.

I'm not sure why she chose me. We'd always been friendly but never exactly friends. Maybe it had something to do with Jack, maybe she just felt she owed me an invitation, or maybe she did ask other people first and they said no. But whatever the reason, I was happy to accept. The truth was that I was a little lonely, and sort of bored. You know, Addy had moved to Montreal in the fall, and I missed her a lot like I always did. And I had always sort of liked Rose because she was like me. There wasn't anything special about either of us really, but now she was better than me because she had really suffered, really lost something. It sounds stupid, but I always thought that people who had suffered a real tragedy in their lives were special somehow, glamorous almost, like they got to feel and understand things the rest of us don't.

Rose's apartment was on the main floor at the back, and there was still a cardboard skeleton hanging on the front door from Halloween—holding its own skull underneath its arm—that they hadn't got around to taking down yet. I guess they had other things on their mind but really, it had been almost a month. I was surprised no one else had taken it down for them if they weren't going to do it themselves.

I rang the bell and Rose's father opened the door, he was dressed in a black suit but without a tie, just like at the funeral, and he took my hand and shook it solemnly, saying, "You must be Natalie, it's a pleasure to meet you." His name was Tim and he hung up my coat for me and put my backpack in Rose's bedroom. Rose was in the kitchen, washing up. Her mother, Janine, was in the bathroom getting dressed up to go.

He was tall and thin, and terribly handsome. He wore his hair down his back in a long braid of grey though he wasn't really old at all, supposedly it had turned grey after a hunting trip up north that had gone horribly wrong, the same trip where he lost the pinky and ring finger off his left hand, but he'd learned to hold his hand so you didn't even notice unless you were looking right at it.

He was a lot like Bethany. He had a way of either talking to you that made you feel like you were the only other person in the room, or ignoring you that made you feel like you didn't even exist. His eyes were dark brown and deep with grief, a grief I liked to believe went back before Bethany died, that it went back even before he lost his fingers and his hair went grey, that went back maybe to before he was even born.

He was kind of vain. He always dressed well and used a little cologne, and Rose said he'd spend hours on his hair. He didn't work. He was apparently on disability, though I don't know why, and he was pretty much constantly drunk—never a *lot* drunk, always just drunk enough. I rarely ever saw him with alcohol. He preferred to do his drinking in secret. Not that I suppose anyone would have tried to stop him or given him a hard time about it, the way Mom used to give Davey a hard time about his beer. I guess he just enjoyed it more that way—they say some people do. This is all stuff I would learn about him later. All I saw at the time was that he talked to me like I was an adult and not a little kid, and that he was far too good-looking for his wife, though clearly he completely adored her. While Tim looked old from a distance, because of his grey hair, and then when you got closer you saw he wasn't really that old at all, with Janine it was just the opposite. From a distance, like when I saw her at the funeral, she practically looked like a kid, like she was our age, I guess because she was so petite and the way she liked to dress. It wasn't until you got closer that you saw the lines around her mouth and eyes and the way her breasts were pretty saggy, the spots on her arms, stuff like that. She was actually older than Tim, by almost five years apparently, yet if you saw them walking together from across the street you might think that they were father and daughter before you'd think they were husband and wife. She wore her hair in a bob, or sometimes with two little pigtails, and she had thick glasses that magnified her eyes so much it made you think of a bullfrog or a fish.

Their apartment smelled like ashtrays and oil paint. Tim apologized for the mess as he showed me in. Half their stuff was in open cardboard boxes, piled here and there along the walls. They were moving at the end of the month, he told me, to a smaller apartment in the same building.

There were only the two bedrooms. The bigger one had been Bethany's and the smaller one was Rose's. Tim and Janine slept on a futon in the living room that folded up into a couch during the day, and they had a thin blue blanket hung on a clothesline that they pulled across like a curtain at night to cut off the room.

What would have been, I guess, the dining room, they used as Janine's studio, with one of those cool slanted drafting tables for her to draw on and an easel for her paintings. I don't really know anything about painting, but Tim talked a lot about how much he admired his wife's great talent, so I assumed they must be good.

I can still close my eyes and see, in perfect detail, the half-finished picture that was propped on the easel that first time I went to their apartment. It was a portrait of Bethany. I knew that because I looked at the photograph she was working from, tacked up next to the easel. The head wasn't painted in yet, just the body and most of the background. She was standing on a city street at night, and I think she was crossing the street but I couldn't tell if she was supposed to be in motion or just standing a little awkwardly, and there was a car there—you could just see the front of its hood sticking into the picture—shining its headlights on her. Her skin was painted green, I don't know why. I never saw the finished picture.

In the kitchen, Rose was just finishing up with the last few dishes. She put the kettle on and told her father that she'd called the taxi for them and it ought to be there in five or ten minutes. I think they were going to some kind of fancy dinner, or something. Anyway, Tim was afraid that he was going to be bored, or boring, or both, and Rose said, "Don't be ridiculous, everybody loves you," in an impatient way, with a touch of contempt even, that kind of surprised me. Then the phone rang to say the cab had arrived, and Janine finally came out of the bathroom, I barely got to meet her, she just introduced herself quickly by the front door while she was putting on her coat and boots. She was wearing the exact same outfit they'd given me for my birthday present, same pattern and colours and everything. It was probably even the same size.

For Christmas that year I bought Rose her own teapot with matching sugar bowl and milk jug. I was terribly into tea that winter, under Rose's influence, and drank tons of it, always Earl Grey with lots of sugar and a little milk, Jack made fun of me for it and Mom threatened to start charging me out of my allowance for all the money she was spending on teabags, but of course she never did.

My Christmas present from Rose was a diary with unlined pages and the covers were real leather, the soft kind. It was so nice I never wrote in it, I wanted to save it for something special, and then it just sat in a drawer untouched.

They had moved into their new apartment, on the opposite side of the building and in the basement. Rose said that when they first moved in she couldn't get a good night's sleep, because there was a car alarm that went off outside her window every night at exactly 1:29 and wouldn't stop until 2:47. It sounded really close, like it must be parked on the street right outside her window, but she often couldn't see any car parked there at all. Her parents said they never heard it.

One night she stayed dressed in bed, awake and waiting, and as soon as the alarm began going off, she snuck outside to try and find it, and, I don't know, slash the tires or key the door or something. She circled around and still couldn't find the right car, and she locked herself out of the building by accident though she could have sworn she'd grabbed her keys, and she had to wake her mother banging on the living room window to let her back in. This was in January.

The window in Rose's bedroom looked out on Euclid Ave, but the snow drifted up against it so you could hardly see out. Her room was a bit bigger than her old bedroom had been, but just a bit. The kitchen was a little bigger too, but there was no dining room, so Tim and Janine had to use the living room as master bedroom, sitting room and painting studio all in one. Other than that, it looked just the same as the old place when I had seen it, right down to the open cardboard boxes piled along the wall that they never did get around to unpacking and putting away, which made me wonder if those same boxes had been sitting around half-packed since they had moved down from Iqaluit five years before. By New Year's the place even smelled like the old apartment, like cigarette smoke and oil paint. It was too cold to have the windows open, and the paint fumes especially got so thick I'd feel high sometimes just hanging out for an hour or two after school.

I wondered what they had done with Bethany's stuff, the stuff out of her old bedroom. Some of it, I was pretty sure, had made its way into Rose's new room, and I know that they must have kept at least some of her clothes and shoes, since Rose started wearing them the next year, but I didn't know that then. And what about the rest of her stuff, her books and her bed and her dresser, and her music and her makeup and everything else she'd owned? Did they throw those out, give them away, stick them in a storage room somewhere? Were there bits and pieces of Bethany's leftovers in those cardboard boxes lining the walls? Or maybe they just left her room and all of the stuff that was in it untouched when they moved out of the old apartment, and just left it the way it was for the caretaker or the new tenants to take what they wanted and get rid of the rest.

I was horribly curious but I never asked. It seemed like a terrible thing to ask someone. I never brought up Bethany at all, I'm too much of a coward, I can't stand to see people cry. I guess I could have been a better friend if only I had been a little braver.

# 4

"I REMEMBER HER," MALCOLM SAID. "YOU REMEMBER EVERYTHING here, that's the worst thing about this place, you can never forget a damn thing. I didn't get to talk to her, though. She ran away from me after I'd helped her. Most people do."

He walked on slowly, treading gently on his blistered feet, and he kept to the middle of the street.

"I can find her," Rose said to him. "If she's here, I can find her."

"There are millions of people here. Millions, tens of millions, hundreds of millions, I don't know. The city goes on for hundreds of miles, it never ends. It's been more than a year now since your sister died. She could be almost anywhere. Then again," he added, with a kind of grim amusement, "you've got the rest of eternity to spend looking for her, don't you?"

"Will you help me?" she asked.

"No," he said curtly, "I won't." He had stopped walking, abruptly, and looked her in the face for the first time since they'd left the church.

"Listen," he said. "You're one of the lucky ones. A lot of people come here, hoping to find someone they love, someone who died before them, and they aren't here." There was pain in his voice and pain in his face. "But you've got someone you *can* find, someone who *is* here. You've got something to hope for."

"Did you..." she started to ask, and then trailed off, uncertain how to phrase the question so it wouldn't be hurtful. But she didn't have to finish it, he answered it anyway.

"I did," he said, turning away and starting to walk once more. "My wife."

Malcolm had been married in 1937, he told her. They had no children and lived in a third-floor flat in London, not far from Stepney Green. They were still trying to get pregnant when he shipped out to fight in the war. The following year her loving cheerful letters stopped reaching him. He learned that their building had been wiped out by German bombs in the first days of the blitz, but her body was never found or identified.

He spent the rest of the war trying to get himself killed and somehow failing even to get injured. All around him people got to die, but Malcolm never did; half the men he fought beside died, men with families at home and something to live for, but the bullets and the bombs kept missing him again and again. Then the war was over and he had nothing left to do but go back to no home and no one, try to drink himself to death and dream of seeing her again.

"It was raining the night I died," he told Rose wistfully. It was the evening before their tenth wedding anniversary and he had gone for a walk, the first time he'd left his room in days. A lovely cool rain on his face, it made him feel clean and peaceful, happy about what he was planning to do.

"It never rains in this place," he told her. "No rain, no snow, no sun, no night, nothing but the wind and the same grey sky forever." Sometimes, he said, he dreamed that it *would* rain here one day and that would mean the world was coming to an end and they would be free.

When he woke up after he died, there was no one to help him or tell him where he was. He knew that he was dead, but that was all he knew. Naked, wet, and bleeding steadily from the deep long slits in his wrists, he had to beg for clothes from the people he met on the streets, and when begging didn't work, he had to use threats and his razor blade. He was so hungry he thought he would go mad, but no one told him that you cannot eat here. He tried eating the leaves off the trees, fistfuls of weeds, even drinking his own blood that still gushed from his cut wrists, but he vomited up everything instantly, leaving him feeling torn up inside, twisted with pain, and just as hungry as ever.

Yet in a way he had been happy at first, for he imagined then that all the dead were here, and if he looked long enough he would find his wife, and they would be reunited. When he finally understood and accepted the truth, that in this city were all the people and only the people who had killed themselves, that they were cut off from the rest of the dead, he cried so hard that if he'd been alive he would have died.

He met a man who had been there for hundreds of years, and who claimed to have met others who had been there for thousands. He met an Argentinean woman who had turned ninety-four years old before she took poison and died, she said she just got tired of waiting.

He became friends with a migrant farm worker who had killed himself after he lost his leg and his livelihood in an accident; he met a man from Kansas who had castrated himself and bled to death in a motel room for reasons he refused to speak of; and a middle-aged Ukrainian woman who was convinced that Malcolm was her long-lost son, and nothing he could say would make her believe the truth.

There were very few children here, the youngest he ever met was eight years old, a shy and quiet little girl who had drowned herself in a lake and she couldn't say why, just that it had seemed quieter down there under the water. The girl's name was Katerina and everyone called her Kitty. She was watched over by a young woman named Alma who'd hanged herself for being seventeen and pregnant, and by a man named Carol who carved a crude wooden doll for her with the knife he'd used to cut his own throat. So there could be kindness even in a place like this, and that made Malcolm hate himself, and want to be alone, until he couldn't bear to be alone any longer.

He told Rose that every time you turned left down a street, it took you closer to the middle of the city, where the buildings were older and more decrepit, the trees larger and closer together, and where the streets were thronged with people who had gone long crazy with pain, misery or hope. The wind, he told her, usually blew in towards the centre of the city and tried to push you that way, but you couldn't trust it, it swirled around sometimes as if on purpose to confuse you. When you turned to the right, it always took you towards the outskirts of the city, where newcomers arrived, and Malcolm spoke to many people who had tried, in their time, to get to the outskirts and somehow get beyond them, to find a way out of the city. All of them gave up eventually. There was no end to the streets, they said, and the city kept expanding as more and more people arrived.

"What if no one committed suicide any more?" Rose asked him. "Then the city wouldn't have to get any larger, and maybe then you could find a way beyond the edge."

"You mean what if no one anywhere ever killed themselves ever again?" he said. "Well, that would be the same thing as the world coming to an end, wouldn't it? So maybe then it'll rain, that would be nice."

They had come to a four-way intersection, and Malcolm stopped. On one corner, there was a crumbling limestone building with black mold eating its way up the walls and a massive clock set at the peak. The brass and ornate hands of the clock clicked heavily as they advanced, but the face of the clock was completely bare, without numbers or markings of any kind.

"You won't come with me?" she asked one last time. "Even a little way?"

"No," he said curtly, "I won't. But good luck to you, Rose. Don't give up. Your sister's out there somewhere, sooner or later you'll find her." He held out his hand to shake hers; she felt a sudden desire to embrace him, but when she moved awkwardly towards him, opening her arms, he shrank back.

Turning to the right, he began to walk away. "Good luck, Rose," he said again, without turning around. "Goodbye."

Gathering up all her courage, Rose turned to the left and started to walk. The street she turned onto was narrower than the one she'd left, with worn cobblestones instead of paved with asphalt. The houses were short and built one right next to the other. They were roofed with red ceramic tiles, and all had peeling, white paint and candy-red window frames, most with the glass smashed out. She had gone no further than fifteen or twenty feet when she turned and looked behind her, but not only was Malcolm gone, the intersection where he'd left her was gone too. The street she was on now stretched out in both directions as far as she could see.

Rose tried walking back the way she came. She walked twenty, forty, fifty feet, and still no intersection. The wind was at her face, blowing cold, and she began to shiver. Her legs felt weak beneath her.

She turned to the left, and then again left at the next intersection. She walked slowly, cautiously, hugging herself for the phantom hope of warmth as the cold wind whipped and slashed at her bare arms and bare legs.

Though she'd been in this place for hours and hours, the sky was the same gloomy unbroken dusk as when she had arrived, and it didn't seem like it would ever change. She had noticed too that nothing in this place cast a shadow—not the people, the trees, the buildings, not even the faintest shadow at all. There was nothing to cast a reflection so she could see her face, and perhaps worst of all, there was no sign or trace of animal life: no birds wheeling across the sky, no dogs barking in the distance. It gave an eerie emptiness to the city, even though it was full of noises. Even beetles or black ants scuttling along the pavement, or a fly buzzing in her face, even that would have been a kind of pleasure for her right now, she thought.

Sometimes, out of the corner of her eye, she would just catch sight of a figure hurrying in the other direction and then disappearing, or of a face looking down at her from one of the windows. But when she turned to look, it would dart out of sight, and when she tried to call out, no one would answer. Down one street she saw a woman with a curiously disfigured face, as though she were wearing a mask of wax and it had partially melted. This woman was sitting on the ground, leaning up against a building and rocking slightly back and forth, but when Rose tried to talk to her, the woman rolled over onto her hands and knees and scurried away with surprising quickness, disappearing around a sudden corner.

She was wearing her sister's tie around her neck, knotted loosely, with the end tucked inside her dress, against her breast. Now and then she lifted her hand to touch it lightly. When she had set out into the snow and the night to die, she had never seriously believed she'd see Bethany again. She had imagined it, a thousand times she had imagined it, but she hadn't really believed it. She hadn't believed in an afterlife at all. All she had hoped for was peace, and perpetual silence. She didn't get it, but if Bethany was here, if they could be together again, then as horrible as this place might be, at least they could have each other.

Rose heard voices coming from somewhere behind her, women's voices, but she couldn't make out any words. The sound seemed distant to her ears, far-off and distorted, but when she turned around Rose discovered that two women were almost upon her, hardly a few feet away. Startled, she backed up quickly, lost her footing, and fell awkwardly to the ground.

The women burst into concerned and excited chatter as Rose stumbled, talking in a language she didn't understand—Spanish, perhaps, or Portuguese. One of the women was short, with a squat thick body, the other tall and stooped. Their hair was black and grey and greasy and dirty, their fingernails cracked and yellow and jagged, their faces wide and brown. They both had gapped and yellow teeth, and blue-black cyanosed lips that give them a sinister, nightmarish appearance.

They advanced quickly on Rose, almost pouncing on her, reaching out their hands and pulling her to her feet. They pawed at her, all the while chattering rapidly to one another, the tall one clucking and the short one cooing. They stroked her hair and caressed her arms, they fingered her dress and Bethany's tie, they brushed her cheeks with the backs of their rough and calloused hands.

It was intolerable, invasive, almost suffocating. She tried pushing their hands away—she yelled at them to stop—but they kept pressing back against her, until finally Rose shoved one of the women so hard she fell, and then Rose turned, and ran. She didn't stop running until she had turned two or three different corners, not even paying attention to what direction she was going.

When she stopped running, she found herself in a maze of narrow alleys between tall blind buildings, windowless and brick, lined with decrepit metal fire escapes that had no windows or doors opening onto them, didn't reach the ground or the roofs, and provided no escape for anyone. Puddles of blood had collected in the corners of the rough uneven street, oily and slick and reeking like rotten meat, and spiky weeds pushed through the cracked and pitted concrete. The wind was gusting and swirling from every direction at once, bringing with it the sound of footsteps that might or might not be hers echoed back.

Every time she reached a turn, she hoped it would open onto a new avenue, but it always brought her to more of the same. The longer she walked through this maze of alleys she had stumbled into, the more turns she took, the narrower her way became, the closer the buildings around her, until they were so close that she could touch the red brick walls on either side of her without even stretching out her arms. She tried turning around and retracing her steps, going back the way she came from, but the alleys continued to become narrower and narrower. An unaccustomed claustrophobia began to weigh on her. She felt something close to panic starting to push at her breast, when she came at last upon a gate, and an end to these streets.

A wrought-iron gate, taller than her, topped with dull and ornamental spikes sat slightly ajar, and creaked loudly as she pushed it open. She stepped into a kind of courtyard, enclosed by twelve-foot stone walls.

Everything here was grey worn stone, flaked and crumbling with age, as if abandoned for centuries. There was an ornamental pool in the middle of the courtyard, but no water in it, only patches of slimy black mildew along the bottom. It was surrounded by a low stone bench and had a statue in the centre that probably would have been a fountain if there were any water to flow through it—a pot-bellied boy holding his penis in one hand, as if to pee in a long high arc. The boy's head had been smashed in, his nose and a piece of his cheek lying in rubble in the mildew at the bottom of the pool. On the far side of the courtyard, near a second wrought iron gate exactly like the one she had entered through, was a fat and blackened tree that someone had torn a branch from, and the blood was still pulsing from the screaming wound, covering the ground.

There was writing on the stone walls surrounding the courtyard. Using the tree's blood for paint, and the branch, perhaps, as a brush, someone had written on the walls, in two-foot dripping letters, a short phrase in several languages: Die Königen ist Angekommen—La Reine est Arrivée—the Queen has Come.

Rose had no idea what it could mean, if it meant anything at all apart from mere insanity, but it filled her with a deep unease. The wind was spinning and howling with a high metallic whine. As she hurried past the fountain towards the far gate, a piece of the boy's left temple and half his eye slid from his face and smashed in the bottom of the empty pool.

As she walked on, Rose found herself constantly turning to look behind her, starting at every noise, as if she were walking down a dark and downtown alley in the dead of night, fearful of attack. She had realized that because none of the streets were as long as they appeared, because crossroads and turnings could suddenly appear at any place and any moment, it meant that people might appear at any moment as well, coming around a corner that wasn't there a second ago, behind her or beside her, just as those two women had.

She began to wonder how she was ever going to find her sister in this place. She pictured herself condemned to wander the streets aimlessly, for years, decades, centuries. She wondered, too, what Bethany was doing and feeling at this moment. Was she wandering aimlessly too, with no hope of ever again seeing the face of someone who loved her? Or was she perhaps holed up in some building, hiding, crying? Rose tried calling out her name, once, twice, three times, listening to her voice get snatched away by the wind. Then someone behind her said, in a voice that sounded like gargling, "Looking for someone?"

Rose jumped, swinging her arm out recklessly as she spun around.

It was an elderly man, elderly but not frail looking. He was dressed in a crumpled brown suit, and had a pale blue shirt swathed in a crude bandage around the back of his head, almost like a turban. The butt of a handgun stuck ostentatiously out from his waistband, and she had a hard time understanding him speak, for he must have killed himself by placing the barrel of the gun inside his mouth and blowing out the back of his head.

"It's all right," he was saying. "It's all right, I'm not going to hurt you." With no roof to his mouth to provide resonance, his words had a hollow, slurred and drowning quality that was hard to decipher and painful to listen to, and he had to turn his head every few seconds and spit out the great welts of blood that collected in his mouth. But his eyes were kind.

Rose's first impulse was to run, but she told herself that if she couldn't find the courage to talk to people, she might as well give up hope of ever finding Bethany. So she forced herself to stand steady and swallow her fear and she said, "Yes. Yes, I'm looking my sister. I know she's here, somewhere...."

He asked her what she looked like, and closed his eyes as if to review in his mind the image of every teenaged girl he had encountered in this city, but he could think of no one who might have been Bethany—at least no one he'd actually spoken to, or who had let him get close enough to get a good look at.

They talked for a while. He had been, he told Rose, a funeral director when he was alive, and now he was wandering in search of the people whom he had embalmed and buried when he was alive, hoping to give them some comfort by describing their funerals to them. He could remember each and every one with utter clarity, and of the thousands he had buried over four decades there were precisely eighty-three that had, to his certain knowledge, died by suicide.

"And does it give them any comfort?" she asked him doubtfully. "I don't know," he admitted, turning to spit. "I've yet to find any. Give me time, they must be here."

This was discouraging, Rose thought. If he hadn't been able to find any one of eighty-three people in all the years he'd been searching, how hard would it be for her to find just one? Like a single needle in a near infinite field of haystacks.

Before they parted ways, the man offered Rose his suit jacket. He could see how cold she was, the way she shivered involuntarily and rubbed her arms, how her eyes and her nose were still running, and she had told him how she had died. She said no, at first, but he insisted, and she knew that it would be unkind not to accept. She thought of what Malcolm had said to her, how there was kindness even in this place, and how it made him hate himself more than ever.

The jacket was much too big for her, so she draped it over her shoulders like a shawl, but no matter how tightly she drew it around herself she felt not even the slightest bit warmer. The freezing cold she felt didn't come from the air around her. It was something she carried inside her own body.

# 5

THAT FIRST MORNING AFTER ADDY ARRIVED I GOT A PHONE call from Rose's mother Janine, totally out of the blue, asking if I had heard from her, or knew where she might be. It was the shortest day of the year, and even though Jack and Addy and I had been up for a while it was still gloomy and dark outside, the snow blowing thick and wicked in the half-light.

The kitchen was freezing. You could feel the cold leeching through the wall, and slipping through the plastic over the window, and creeping under the door from the mudroom. I was sitting at the kitchen table, my feet up on a chair and a blanket wrapped around me, trying to coax Typhus, Jack's big fat cat, to jump up in my lap and help keep me warm.

Jack was standing over the stove, ladling pancake batter into one frying pan, prodding the bacon in another, and trying not to trip over Typhus, who was winding his lumpy orange body around his ankles. The stupid cat adored Jack, he was completely devoted to him. Me, he pretty much tolerated, he'd even let me pet him sometimes if Jack wasn't around. But Addy he absolutely hated. She hated him, too, she said he was a thief, a liar, a tattletale, and a slut.

Jack had taken him in when he was just a scrawny orange kitten with a bare patch on his back and big flappy ears, all crawling with mites. He'd rescued him from a pack of first-graders who had him stuck up a tree and were hucking gravel at him. This was when we were still living in that apartment on Jarvis, and you weren't supposed to have any pets allowed at all, but Jack smuggled him in inside his jacket. He wanted to name the cat Lantern, but the week after Jack adopted him, me, Jack and Mom all got wicked sick, and spent two days puking and crapping all over the apartment. It probably wasn't the cat's fault at all. It was probably just a coincidence, but Mom and I blamed him anyway and started calling him Typhoid Mary, only later we shortened that to Typhus because it really isn't fair to call a male cat Mary, even if he did give you killer diarrhea.

Mom and Davey were just getting out of bed. You could hear them above our heads, floorboards creaking under Mom's weight as she moved around. Addy was perched on the kitchen counter, her butt by the sink and her foot in the butter. She always did like sitting on countertops instead of chairs. She said it gave her a better view. And she was sipping from her second cup of coffee, a habit she must have picked up in Montreal.

"Hey, so this is weird," she said. "Did anyone else hear someone knocking on the front door at two in the morning?"

I shook my head.

"I know *you* didn't," she said. "You were snoring away, I couldn't even wake you. Did you know you snore?"

"Oh, whatever. I don't snore."

"What about you?" she asked Jack. "Did you hear it?" He shook his head too. "Man, you guys sleep through everything."

"So," I prompted her, "somebody knocked on the door at two in the morning...."

"Right," she said, "and this is the thing. I didn't want to open the door cause I figured it was probably just some drunk, right? But then I thought, what if it's someone who needs help, and it's snowing outside and everything. And then they knocked again, and I looked out the window and *there was no one there*."

Jack shrugged. "Probably just a tree branch or something."

"So I opened the door and looked out," Addy went on enthusiastically, ignoring him, "and there was no one there, no one anywhere on the street in sight at all. But get this, there were footprints in the snow going up the walk, up the stairs to the door, but there weren't any footprints going away. They just led up to the door and disappeared!" She paused a moment to let the full effect of her story sink in. "Freaky, eh?"

"Okay," said Jack, "I'm calling bullshit. You either made that up or dreamed it or something."

"Nuhn-unh."

"Then okay, show me the footprints."

"No good," said Addy cheerfully, "I checked already, the snow's all covered them up."

"Of course it has," he said. "Very convenient."

"Hey, go ahead, don't believe me. We'll ask Nora when she comes down, maybe she heard the knocking. She was up all night peeing, anyway. You know how many times I heard her get up to go to the bathroom? Six times," she said. "I counted," she added, I guess in case we thought she might be exaggerating. "Six times."

I was pretty sure she was exaggerating.

She appealed to Jack. "You must have heard her, right?"

But Jack sleeps like he's dead anyway, and he made like he was too busy concentrating on not burning his pancakes and just ignored her.

Above us, we could hear the toilet getting flushed again.

"Well, I'll tell you what I think," said Addy. "I think she's going into labour, that's what I think."

"I don't know," I said. " Just cause she had to pee all night? That's been going on for a while."

"Sure," said Addy, "But look at how it's snowing outside."

That's when the phone began to ring. It rang twice, and no one made any move to go and answer it. It rang a third time, and Jack said, "Isn't someone going to get that?"

"It's not my house," said Addy. It rang a fourth time.

"It's never for me anyway," I said.

"Well, I'm kind of busy here," said Jack irritably, gesturing at the frying pan with the spatula as the phone rang a fifth time. He sounded just like Mom, it was funny.

"They'll leave a message," I said. The sixth ring was a half ring, meaning it had clicked over to voicemail, and I said, "See?" But instead of leaving a message, they must have hung up and dialed right back, because after ten or fifteen seconds it started to ring again, and this time Davey yelled down from the top of the stairs, "Will somebody down there answer the damn phone, please?" He sounded pretty edgy.

"Typhus," I said, "Come here, Typhus." I narrowed my eyes and rubbed my fingertips together and said, "Pssstpsstpsst," like I'd heard you're supposed to do when you're trying to beckon a cat. Not that it ever worked.

"Fine," said Jack angrily, moving the frying pan off the hot element with a clatter. He stomped into the living room to find the phone.

We heard him answer it and then, after a moment, say, "Yes she is, just a minute please." He came back into the kitchen with a smug and martyrous look on his face, and handed it to me.

"Natalie," said the voice. "It's me, Janine." She said it as though we had last spoken just a few days before, not eight months ago. And I had maybe the strangest sensation I've ever experienced. The past rushed back at me. It seemed like just yesterday that Rose and I were close and spoke all the time; but then at the same time it seemed very long ago, a lot longer than just a year, if that makes any sense at all. And the skin on the back of my neck was prickling, and it prickled all up and down my back. God knows I'm not psychic or anything remotely like it, but at that moment I knew, just knew, what she was going to say and what it meant.

Addy told me later that I turned white and started to shiver a little. I don't think I was conscious of it at the time, but I was aware that Jack and Addy were staring at me as Janine told me that Rose had snuck out of the apartment last night, and had I seen her? Had I heard from her? Did I know where she might have gone? Outside the house, the wind was howling and whipping the snow against the window. Inside the house, I could hear Mom's footsteps coming down the stairs.

I didn't explain to Janine that I never talked to Rose any more, I just said politely that I didn't know and promised to call if I heard anything at all.

"Are you all right?" said Addy as I put down the phone.

"What the hell was that about?" said Jack.

But I just shook my head and said, "I'll tell you later."

"Tell us what later?" asked Mom, waddling into the kitchen. She looked all pasty and strung out, and she glared at Addy, who quickly took her foot down off the counter and said, "Good morning, Nora. Did you have a good sleep?"

"Good morning, Addy. You shouldn't wear your cap inside the house, it's very rude. And Natalie," she added, turning back on me, "take your feet off the chair, how many times do I have to tell you? And stop chewing your nails."

"Sorry, Nora," Addy said, sliding down off the counter and taking off her cap. "Cup of coffee?"

"Sorry, Nora," I said, pulling down my feet, sweeping the nonexistent dirt off the seat, and then moving the chair back to its place.

"I'd love a cup, thank you Addy," said Mom. "And you," she said to me, "Don't call me Nora."

"Who was on the phone?" said Davey as he came into the room. He looked sleep-deprived too, with dark bags under his eyes, but he also seemed suspiciously cheerful.

I said, "Addy thinks Mom is in labour."

"I'm not in labour," Mom snapped. She was walking very carefully over to the table, trying not to spill her coffee, which Addy had filled the cup a little too full.

"I think she might be in labour," said Davey. He went to pour himself a cup of coffee, but there was only a dribble left at the bottom of the pot.

"I'm not in labour," said Mom, almost yelling. She had just reached the table, but before she could put her cup down, she had some kind of spasm, sucking her breath in sharply, grabbing the back of the chair with her free hand as she bent over, and sloshing half her coffee over the floor and my feet.

I took the cup out of her hand and put it on the table. Addy tossed a dishcloth at me to wipe up the spill. Mom just stood there, bent over and holding on to the back of the chair and the table, breathing torturously in and out through her mouth. I don't know how long it lasted, maybe twenty seconds, half a minute? More? I don't know, it felt like a really long time. Davey's eyes were flicking back and forth between Mom and his wristwatch. When her body finally relaxed, and she started breathing normally again, he mouthed the words, "I think she's in labour," careful not to make a sound.

"I'm not in labour," said Mom angrily, just as if she'd heard him anyway. She twisted her head around, still leaning on the back of the chair. "Who here's had a baby before? Have you ever given birth, Davey? What about you, Addy? Have you had a lot of babies? Jack? Natalie? All right then, *I'll* tell you when I'm in labour."

And then she said, "Ah, *shit*," in a different tone of voice, and Davey said, "Oh hell, oh hell, oh hell." Jack scrunched up his face in disgust and Addy gave a little excited leap, clapping her hands four quick quiet times in front of her face.

From where I was sitting I couldn't see it at first, what all the excitement was about, but her water had broken, running down both legs and dripping onto the floor to form a little pool. "Okay," Mom said. "Now I'm in labour maybe."

Addy was turning pirouettes in the middle of the kitchen floor, chanting, "I knew it, I knew it!"

Davey turned grey and ran away. Jack looked sick, and so did Mom. Her face had gone all blotchy and red and she said to me, very, very sweetly, "Natalie, honey, could you get a towel for the floor?" And then she added, much louder and with a really startling amount of ferocity, "*Shut* up, Addy."

I helped Mom lower herself into her chair, and then Addy tossed a couple dishtowels to me. Typhus had sneaked over to the pool of womb juice on the floor and was sniffing it tentatively, as if trying to decide whether to start lapping it up, which was completely disgusting and I had to snap one of the towels at him to chase him away.

"Davey," Mom started to say, and then stopped. "Where'd Davey go?"

"He ran upstairs," said Addy.

"Idiot," said Mom. "Jack, will you go outside for me and start the car? My keys should be in my purse. By the front door."

Jack nodded weakly, and scampered off to get on his boots and coat, just throwing them on over his pajamas. Outside it was still snowing, though the wind was blowing and swirling it around so much, it was hard to tell how much was actually coming down and how much just blowing around.

After I had cleaned up the puddle as best I could, I asked Mom if I could make another cup of coffee for her, or get her anything, anything at all.

"Do you want some bacon?" Addy asked. She had snatched a piece out of the frying pan and was munching on it as she spoke.

Mom's face went kind of greenish-yellow when Addy mentioned bacon, and I thought for a minute she was going to throw up, but instead she started doing that weird breathing thing they teach pregnant women to do. She pulled herself to her feet and then leaned on me, one hand squeezing my shoulder, the other one squeezing my hand. Hard.

When she relaxed her body and let go of my hand, Addy announced, "Thirty-eight seconds."

Davey appeared in the kitchen doorway, fully dressed now and holding a big pile of Mom's clothes in his arms. "Thirty-eight seconds," he repeated. "Are you sure?"

"I counted," said Addy.

He looked at his watch, frowning. "When did it start?"

"Thirty-eight seconds before I said, 'thirty-eight seconds.'"

Outside we could hear the car trying to turn over and failing weakly—once, twice, three times it failed, and then on the fourth try it finally caught. The look of relief on Davey's face was pretty funny, but Addy looked disappointed and she didn't try to disguise it.

"I brought you down a bunch of clothes to choose from," Davey said, plopping them down on the kitchen table and kissing Mom anxiously on the top of her head. "Do you want a glass of water? You should drink a glass of water. Natalie, get your mom a glass of water, will you?"

I got her a glass of water.

Jack came in the back door, bringing a blast of cold air with him, covered with a light dusting of white and looking worried. "I don't know," he said. "There's a lot of snow piled up back there."

"Well," said Mom, "start shovelling. Shovel the whole goddamn back lane if you have to."

He nodded once more, and hurried back out.

"Natalie," Mom said, "go help your brother shovel. You too, Addy. Everyone get out of here so I can get dressed."

"Me too?" said Davey.

"No, you idiot," she snapped. "Not you." She looked at me and she looked at Addy. "Go, get," she said. "Go help him."

"But we only own one shovel," I pointed out.

"Then use a spoon," she yelled.

We went.

It was bitterly cold. The wind was brutal, and the snow was like little needles of ice that swirled up and stung you in the face. I went over and borrowed a shovel from the neighbour's back porch, normally I would have asked them but I didn't want to disturb them, it was still pretty early for a Saturday morning, and anyway, this was kind of an emergency, they wouldn't mind.

Addy wasn't dressed warmly enough to help anyway. All she had was one of Davey's sweaters over her thin black jacket and that toque from Tante Martìne, so she just sat in the car, listening to the radio and sticking her head out occasionally to yell words of encouragement, or tell us the weather report, until her nose began to bleed and she had to go back inside.

# 6

ROSE HURT. HER STOMACH WAS TWISTED AND CRAMPED WITH hunger, her tongue and lips and throat were cracked dry and sore from thirst. Her feet and legs ached from the constant walking, and waves of exhaustion were washing over her. Her fingers and nose and ears and toes were frozen, still, bitten and stiff, and no matter how long she walked, she knew she would never warm up—just as the slits in Malcolm's wrists were still bleeding freely seven decades after his death.

She walked along a broad and gently curving street lined with wide, low bungalows, not unlike the suburbs she knew from home. The houses on this street even had lawns, matted with thick tangles of purple thistle growing almost as high as her knees.

So exhausted it was getting hard to think clearly, she decided to make her way into one of the houses and try to sleep. Standing at the edge of the thistles, she tentatively pushed one down with the toe of her boot, breaking the stalk. It oozed a sticky, purple blood, and whimpered like a small and beaten dog. The wind scoured along the ground here as hard as ever, but the thistles were too thick and tangled to do more than sway very slightly. She started making her way carefully across the lawn towards the window of the nearest house, tramping the thistles down with her boots in a wide and careful path ahead of her, occasionally stopping to look back and see if anyone was watching or approaching.

When she reached the house, she found the window was a little higher than she had thought. She could just barely see over the sill. The glass was already broken out and lay in jagged nasty pieces amid the weeds. There were swirls of blood on the windowsill but no one inside the small bare room, and when she tried calling out there was no answer, except in the wind at her back.

She took the jacket from her shoulders and draped it over the sill, half in and half out of the room, and then tried to pull herself up. It took several attempts, but she managed at last to get her elbows over the sill and hoist her body up.

The room was almost exactly like the one that Rose had first arrived in—small, bare and barren, with no door or other exit. The light was slightly dimmer inside the room than it was out on the street. It was a relief to get away from the cold and constant wind, and from the incessant moans and cries the wind carried.

There was some blood on the floor in one corner, still wet, though she knew it could be years old for all that. The urge to get down on her knees like a dog and lap the blood up off the floor was almost overpowering. She was so hungry, so thirsty, but she remembered how Malcolm had warned her about eating and drinking.

Curling up in a corner and hoping that she couldn't be seen from the street, she balled up the jacket for a pillow, lay down her head, and tried to sleep. *Perhaps*, she thought, *this is all a dream, a terrible nightmare, and when I wake up I won't be dead at all, I'll be at home in my bed.* But she didn't really believe it.

The moment she closed her eyes, a memory welled up in her mind of her and her sister sharing a bed in their home up north one night when the heat went out for several hours. They were huddling together under the covers and giggling. The memory was so vivid and insistent that the tears poured out from her eyes, and then her mind was flooded with memories—vivid perfect memories of her childhood, her sister, her life in Iqaluit. The memory of discovering Bethany's body hanging in the closet, memories of the funeral, memories of her father and mother, memories of her friends. Happy memories and horrible ones, all crashing over her in chaotic uncontrollable waves, and instead of sleeping, she sobbed. She cried so hard it physically hurt; her body twisted, it clenched like a fist. She gasped for air and soaked the jacket with her tears.

Rose had no idea how long she lay there, sobbing, but when she finally summoned up the strength to open her eyes, to sit up first and then climb to her feet, she swore that she would never try to sleep again. She wouldn't even let herself stop and think. She'd walk, just walk, until she found Bethany, and then at least if she had to cry, they could cry together.

She gathered up the tear-soaked jacket and went back to the window, only to find herself looking out on a completely different street than the one she had left. Gone were the rows of low wide bungalows and yards of purple thistle. The very house she was in had changed with her inside it, though the room looked exactly the same, even down to the blood smeared on the windowsill. But the biggest shock of all was to discover that she was now on the second floor once more, with no way of getting down.

She looked out from the second-storey window onto a cobblestone street with tall black trees like scorched and barren oaks. The buildings were wooden, shabby, crowded and decrepit, leaning at precarious angles over the street or against one another. Shingles, gutters and bricks from crumbling chimneys lay in the street as if a great storm had passed through.

The buildings looked more like abandoned shops or hotels than houses, with blank and wooden signboards extending over the doors. Wooden shutters flapped noisily in the gusting wind, creaking and slapping. Some hung by a single twisted hinge, and some had fallen to the street, smashed into splinters. Up the way, one of the trees had grown so close to a building that two of its thickest limbs had broken right through the wall, and it had actually lifted the whole structure a foot or more off its foundations as the tree continued to grow.

She wasn't, she thought, quite as high up from the ground as she had been in the apartment block where she'd first arrived—perhaps fifteen feet up instead of twenty—but it was still too high to safely jump. And then, she was beginning to suspect that distances could be misleading in this place, and that fifteen feet could easily change to twenty or thirty even as she was falling. She had the necktie, but if she tied it to the window frame to try and lower herself down a bit, it would only give her a foot or two more at most, and she wasn't willing to leave it behind.

As she was leaning out to examine the front of the building, trying to think of a way to get safely down, she heard someone call out for help. She looked up and down the street, and in the windows of the buildings around her, but could see no one. Again came the cry for help, a boy's voice, pained and strangulated, and she wondered if it was just the wind playing tricks on her. She tried calling back, yelling, "Where are you? I can't see you."

"Under the tree."

And sure enough, at the base of a tree about seventy or eighty feet to her right, out in the middle of the street, she could just make out somebody standing with his back pressed flat against the trunk. She could see only a pair of bare legs and a glimpse of his face, for the rest of him was hidden by the thick low branches.

"I need your help," she called out to him.

"I need *your* help," he called back.

"I can't get down."

"I can't move," he yelled helplessly. "They tied me here."

Rose didn't answer immediately. She wondered who "they" were and why they had tied the boy to the tree. She wondered, even, if it would be safe to untie him. Perhaps he was dangerous, and they had tied him there for their own protection, or perhaps he was a kind of decoy, like a tethered goat to lure a tiger.

Maybe, she thought, she should wait until another person came along who could help them both. Sooner or later someone would surely come. Or maybe she should just go back in her corner, curl up and try to sleep again, hoping that when she got back up, she'd be on yet a different street in a different house, perhaps with a window closer to the ground. But she couldn't do that. Not only would she hate herself for simply abandoning the boy and not even trying to help him, she couldn't bear the thought of lying down and closing her eyes again.

There were two kinds of pain in this place, both always there and always biting into you, the pain in your body and the pain of your memories; of the two, at that moment, Rose believed that the memories were by far the worse, and that she would rather take the risk of breaking her legs or even her neck, whatever agony that might end up being, than to lie down and close her eyes and let those memories come rushing freely back.

"Please," called the boy again, breaking the long uneasy silence. "Please help me."

"I *will* help you," she called back. "I just have to figure out how I can get down from here. You're tied to the tree? With a rope?"

"Yes."

"I could use a rope," she said, leaning out and looking up now, towards the roof.

"Untie me and you can have it."

"Can I have it first and untie you after?"

She wondered if she could possibly climb up onto the roof. It was almost flat, just a gradual slope, and from there she could easily leap to the roof of the next building over—there was only a foot or two gap between them—and then onto the roof next to that, the building with the tree growing through it. Even with her hands frozen and stiff, she felt confident that she could climb down that tree, if only she could get onto the roof and get to it.

Before she climbed out the window, she took the suit jacket and dropped it to the street. Then she carefully pulled herself up onto the sill and slowly stood, facing in towards the building. Her knees began to shake slightly. She stood there motionless, forcing herself to breathe deeply and slowly until the steadiness came back to her legs.

Her head was just below the overhang of the roof, which extended perhaps three or four inches out past the wall, and then another two inches for a rusted and unpainted eavestrough that ran the length. She knew she wouldn't have the arm strength to simply pull herself up without any help, but there was a second window to her left that still had its shutters attached—one latched, one banging freely back and forth in the breeze—that she thought perhaps she could use to climb up on. It didn't seem likely that the shutters would bear her weight, but she wouldn't have to put all her weight on them anyway, and she thought that if she could go quickly, she might get away with it. Anyway, she had to try something, and it was the only possibility she could think of.

Holding on to the eavestrough with both hands, she started to inch her way along the windowsill. There was a two-foot gap from window to window, and as she carefully stretched her left leg across that gap, she very nearly fell when the eavestrough began to pull free of the roof, just that little bit of extra weight she had placed on it. She pulled her foot back to the sill, got her right arm inside the window, and pulled her body flat against the wall, heart beating wildly.

She took a few more slow deep breaths and began inching her way back to the other side of the windowsill, near the edge of the building. She knew now that there was simply no way she could get safely up onto the roof, but she had another idea.

Rose carefully maneuvered herself around so that she was facing out onto the street, and then holding onto the window with her left arm she reached up with the right, got a firm grip on the eavestrough, and gave it a hard yank, pulling it more out than down. The nails tore free of the rotted wood.

Holding on to the end of the trough with both hands, she pulled it down towards herself, ripping another foot or two out from the wall and bending the thin metal tube. She carefully wiggled and worked the rusted nails out and tossed them into the room behind her, through the window; then she wrapped her arms around the length of crumpled metal, hugged it to her breast, and quickly, before she lost her nerve, she leapt out and down to the street.

Just as she had hoped, the eavestrough pulled free from the building as she swung down, the nails in the wood offering just enough resistance to slow her fall slightly. As soon as she felt her feet touch the ground she let go of the trough and rolled awkwardly, sprawling across the pavement as fragments of wood and shingle rained down over her.

Rose sat up slowly, a little dazed from the adrenalin and winded from the impact, but essentially uninjured. She could hear the boy calling out to her, trying to say something to her, but the blood was pounding in her ears and she couldn't make out the words. The palm of her left hand was cut from where she'd squeezed the metal edge of the eavestrough, and her hip and shoulder were scraped and bruised from the impact with the ground, but there was no major damage—nothing broken, nothing sprained. The eavestrough dangled precariously from one corner of the roof, creaking as it swayed back and forth.

Getting gingerly to her feet, Rose looked around. There was still no one in the street except for her and the boy, who was looking at her now with wide and amazed blue eyes. She went and gathered up the suit jacket before she approached him. He was wearing a plain black shirt that was plastered wet against his skin. He wasn't, she saw, completely naked from the waist down, he had on a pair of raggedy white underwear, and they were wet too, you could see the skin right through them. He was tied to the tree by a rope around his throat; his hands were free, and she tossed him the jacket as soon as she got close enough. He blushed ferociously as he whispered, "Thanks," and he held the jacket over his legs and waist, though not before she got a good look at the ugly bruises, purple and black fat bruises, on his thigh and his hip. There was a small puddle of sour and creamy yellow vomit on the ground, not far from where he stood.

He looked young, perhaps twelve or thirteen at the very most, too young to have killed himself. But here he was. He was a little chubby, soft looking, with smooth, pale skin and light brown hair, soaking wet in short tight curls. He had been tied to the thick trunk of the tree by the throat, tight enough to bite into the skin, with a blue and nylon rope perhaps a quarter of an inch thick.

"Who would do this to you?" Rose asked him as she struggled to loosen the knots at the back of the tree. It was difficult work and slow going with her sore, stiff fingers, but at last she got them loose. The rope fell slack and the boy slumped down to sit at the base of the tree, coughing until he brought up a little gout of water, dribbling down his chin.

"Are you all right?" Rose asked, coming around to his side. It was, she realized immediately, an idiotic question—of course he wasn't all right, he was *here*—but the boy just said, "I'm not crying, I'm not." He wiped the tears away with the heel of his hand and sniffed aggressively as he looked up at her, and then quickly looked away again.

"Okay," she said. "That's okay. You're not crying. What's your name?"

"Emmanuel," he told her, and he thanked her again.

She turned her back to him and walked a little ways away, pretending to be looking up and down the street to see if anyone was coming, so that he could get up from the ground and put the jacket on. It came down past his knees, covering him nicely, but the sleeves were far too long, dangling idiotically almost a foot past his hands. She helped him roll them up as best they could. It would have to do.

"My name's Rose," she said, gathering the rope from the ground. It was a good, strong rope, about ten feet long. "You should always hang yourself," she said quietly to herself. "Then you're still dead, but at least you have the rope."

Emmanuel looked confused. She asked him again what had happened, and who had done this to him.

It was a man and a woman, he told her. They had seemed so nice at first, even though they couldn't speak English very well. At least, the woman couldn't. The man maybe could, but he had apparently hanged himself so he didn't talk much at all, and when he did it was a strained and choking sound, difficult to understand.

The woman had been young, in her early twenties, maybe, young and small. She looked, Emmanuel said naively, like an elf or a faerie, lovely and delicate and graceful. All she had on was a short and flimsy nightgown, powder blue and practically see-through.

The man had looked older, maybe ten or fifteen years older than her, and they had offered Emmanuel some food.

"Food?" Rose interrupted him. They were walking now as they talked, looking for an intersection, trying to get away from the incessant din of the shutters creaking and slapping in the wind.

Emmanuel blushed again. "Sort of," he said, sounding miserable, embarrassed and small. He had tried eating before, he told her, leaves from the trees and stuff like that. He knew what happened when you tried to eat here, but the woman had assured him that this would be different, that this kind of food he'd be able to hold down, and he was just so hungry he couldn't resist the temptation.

So he tried it, but his stomach began to seize and cramp, same as always, he dropped to his hands and knees to vomit, and while he was down on the ground throwing up like a dog, the man had come behind him and looped the rope around his throat and hauled him to his feet, pulling him to the tree and tying him there. They took his shoes, his socks and his pants. He'd tried to fight them off at first, but he was weakened from the vomiting, and the man kicked him four or five times as hard as he could, and threatened to do worse if the boy continued to struggle. The woman put on Emmanuel's clothes and shoes, even though they were all wet, arguing vociferously with the man in some foreign language—Polish or Russian, perhaps.

"I think she wanted him to untie me," Emmanuel said, "so they could take the rope with them, and he didn't want to. He was probably afraid of what I'd do to them," he added, with a weak attempt at bravado, sliding his gaze furtively across to Rose's face.

"What sort of food was it?" she asked him again.

It was, he admitted—almost writhing with embarrassment—breast milk. The woman had given birth, she'd told him, just days before killing herself; the baby hadn't survived, but she was still lactating, just as she had been when she died.

"He was a boy," she had said tenderly. "Maybe grow up like you, if he lived." And then she had uncovered one breast and squeezed it gently to show him the beads of milk emerge from around the nipple.

# 7

WHEN I WAS SIX, I GOT TO BE THE FLOWER GIRL AT MY AUNT Tracy's wedding, out in Neepawa. There's a picture of me, framed and up in the hall by the bathroom door, with my chubby red face looking all fierce like I'm going into battle, and squeezing that bouquet so hard in my little fist I squashed all the stems to a pulp. They were roses, red and pink, and I wore a lilac dress with a dark purple sash and a hairpiece like a tiara of little imitation pink and red roses. Aunt Tracy is Mom's baby sister. She and Uncle Anthony moved out to Calgary a couple years after they got married so we hardly ever see them, I've got two cousins who were born out there and I've only even met them once.

Addy was there at the wedding with us. I don't remember why exactly cause her mother wasn't, so Addy must have been living with us at the time. Casey might have been out tree-planting somewhere. It might have been her last year doing that. Anyway, Addy was there, but she and Jack weren't involved in the ceremony at all, only me, and that was the only wedding any of us had ever been to.

So back when Mom and Davey first started getting really serious, and I told Addy that they'd been talking about him moving in with us, Addy had said, "Hey, they should get married, then I could be the flower girl."

Mom, who was doing something in the kitchen at the time, called out, "I can hear you two, you know," but we just ignored her.

I said, "What are you talking about? You're way too old to be a flower girl." She must have been twelve by then, she had even started wearing a training bra though I don't think she really needed it.

"I'd make a great flower girl," Addy said. "I wouldn't drop the flowers or eat them or anything."

"Flower girls are supposed to be cute little kids with chubby little stubby legs and stuff. You can't have a flower girl who's starting to get breasts, it's bad luck, everybody knows that."

"You're just jealous," said Addy, discreetly adjusting her bra strap. "Anyway, your mom doesn't know any cute little girls with fat legs. What's she gonna do, rent one for the wedding? Snatch some fat-legged toddler off the playground?"

"Well, if anyone's gonna be Mom's flower girl it oughta be me. I'm younger than you *and* I have experience."

"Hey," Mom barked, coming and standing in the doorway. "No one's going to be my flower girl. No flower girls. None, nothing."

"Well," said Addy thoughtfully, "I guess I could be a bridesmaid, then. It's not like your mom has that many friends."

"Hey!" said Mom, almost yelling now. "No flower girls, no bridesmaids, no wedding, end of conversation. Over. Done."

When Mom and Davey had first told us they were pregnant, I remember I felt relieved more than anything—at least at first.

For weeks the two of them had been arguing all the time, even more than normal. What's more, they had been closing their bedroom door and lowering their voices when they argued so we couldn't hear what they were arguing about, which meant it had to be serious. Mom had broken out in red and white pimples on her chin and was sulking around the house, silently glaring at Davey like someone who has been deeply insulted and is trying to suck it up. Davey, on the other hand, seemed even more cheerful than usual, and I kept catching him smirking at us for no apparent reason, so it didn't seem like they were going to break up—or why was he acting so smug about it? He was the one who'd have to move out and have nowhere to live. But I couldn't imagine what it might be.

So when they sat us around the breakfast table one morning and told us they had something important to talk to us about, I felt a tight little knot of fear in my stomach and I didn't want to hear it. And then when Davey said, "We're going to have a baby," I was so relieved and so surprised, I blurted out, "That's disgusting!"

"Natalie!" said Davey, slapping the table. "That's not the point."

Jack, in his serious way, said to Mom, "Are you gonna be okay?"

"Of course I'm going to be okay," Mom said irritably.

"This is happy, exciting news," said Davey.

"I don't want you to go around telling everybody," Mom added abruptly, as if she had just thought of it.

"You kids should be happy and excited about it," Davey complained. "A new little brother or sister to love."

"We'll tell people when we feel like telling people, okay?" said Mom. "You just leave the telling to us."

"Does this mean you're going to get married?" asked Jack.

"Well…" Davey said, giving Mom a sort of speculative look out of the corner of his eyes, but she just said, very firmly, "No, it doesn't mean we're getting married."

"What if it's twins?" I asked.

"It's not twins," said Mom.

"How do you know? It could be twins."

"If it's twins," said Davey, "We'll love them twice as much."

"It's not twins," said Mom. "That's it, end of conversation. Now eat your breakfast."

That night I phoned Addy to tell her the news. "Dammit," she said, "*My* mom never gets pregnant. Is she sure? It could be menopause."

My mom was thirty-five. "I don't think it's menopause," I said.

"Or a tumor, maybe it's a tumor."

"I don't know," I said doubtfully, "I don't think Mom would have said anything if she wasn't *really* sure."

"You're probably right," she admitted. "Nora wouldn't, would she? Hey, maybe now he knocked her up, they'll actually get married."

"Yeah, probably not."

"They *could* get married."

"Honestly, I don't think Mom likes weddings or something."

"Who doesn't like weddings? Everybody likes weddings. Just tell her if she *does* get married, I have to be the maid-of-honour. Remind her that time she promised me."

By the end of our phone call, she had already made her plans to come stay with us over the Christmas holidays and hopefully maybe be there for the birth. All we had to do was convince my mother, convince her mother, and figure out how to find the money for a ticket.

"Maybe it'll be twins," she said, just before we hung up. "That would be cool."

"I think it *is* twins," I said.

Addy was a twin once. My mom and Addy's mother Casey used to be very close friends growing up, almost like sisters, they always did everything together. So when they were eighteen and Mom got pregnant with Jack, Casey went out and got pregnant as well. Then when Mom went into labour, Casey went into labour too, two and a half months premature. She had twins. One of them was born dead, with the umbilical cord wrapped around her little neck, and she named her Madeline. The one that lived she named Adelaide. Which Addy used to complain about, because Casey had picked the names before they were born—as soon as she found out she was having twin girls: Madeline Emilia Mack and Adelaide Elena Mack, Addy and Maddy.

"But how did she know which one I was supposed to be?" Addy would always complain to me. "What if she gave me a dead girl's name by mistake? That's just gross."

Every pregnancy is different, Mom told me. She had morning sickness with Jack at the beginning, but not with me. With Jack she could hardly sleep, especially the last few months. He kicked and rolled so much inside her, and then when she did sleep she had wicked nightmares to wake her up where she was either being suffocated or drowning. But with me she slept all the time, she used to fall asleep any time of the day, anywhere she was sitting, even on the bus or in the middle of a conversation.

With Jack her back hurt, with me it was her feet; with Jack she broke out in zits and ate like a starving dog. Mostly she craved chocolate, but also salty meats like bacon, ham, and pepperoni sticks. With this new baby it was seafood she was always craving, especially shrimp, she ate more shrimp over those eight or nine months than I think she'd eaten in her entire life up till then. When she was carrying me she didn't have any cravings at all. She said she had wicked heartburn the whole time and she could only stomach a handful of really bland things. She mostly lived off milk and white rice and Jack's baby food.

She also used to get gas pains with me that hurt so bad they would twist her up and bend her down and take her breath away, until she could finally fart it out and relieve some of the pressure, and then those farts were so loud and long and toxic that she wished she could die, and she was terrified to leave the house in case it happened in public. She would apparently fart the entire time she'd be asleep, as well. She wouldn't feel any gas pains or discomfort when she was sleeping, but she'd wake up sometimes and the air around her would be practically yellow. I knew that our father had taken off when Mom was pregnant with me, and I wondered now if it was all the farting that was the final straw. If it was half as disgusting as Mom described it, it might have driven me away too.

There was no farting with her third pregnancy, thank God. There were some zits at first, but they cleared up by the end of the summer. Mostly with this one it was the morning sickness, and that never stopped. Which made me kind of worried that it must be a boy, because she'd had the acne and the puking with Jack, but not with me.

I had always assumed that morning sickness meant, you know, being sick in the morning, but apparently they just call it that to confuse people. Mom would go off any time of the day or night. A lot of times there was no warning, she'd seem perfectly fine one moment and then something would set her off, it could be anything at all, and she'd just lean forward and puke all over the place, just like that; then she'd wipe her mouth and gargle some water and she was fine again.

Anything could do it—cheap perfume, dirty dishes sitting in the sink, cigarette smoke on someone's clothes, the smell of Jack's gym shoes, sometimes nothing at all. One time she puked in the car while she was making a left turn through a busy intersection, it went all over the windshield and the dashboard and steering wheel, it's a miracle she didn't crash the car and kill us all. This was in the winter too, and it took Davey an hour and a half to clean it up, out there in the freezing cold. I felt so bad for him.

She threw up on Typhus one time when he'd been sitting on her lap, and he couldn't get away fast enough. We couldn't take him outside to hose him off because it was the middle of winter so we had to take him into the bathtub and turn the shower on him, Jack got scratches all over both arms and I got one nasty scratch down my right cheek that bled like a bugger.

But the worst time by far was when she actually puked into our fridge. She was rooting around in there, looking for something at the back—a jar of pickles, I think—and she came across a bag of rotting lettuce that who knows how long it had been sitting back there, and it had gone all brown and slimy and she just barfed all over everything. It was a catastrophe. The three of us spent the whole afternoon taking everything out of the fridge and scrubbing it down with vinegar and water, and three quarters of our food we had to throw out.

She had her ultrasound in September, early September. The appointment was for eleven o'clock on a Wednesday morning, and she asked me if I wanted to skip school that day so I could come along. That surprised me, but of course I said yes.

It also surprised me that Davey wasn't going. I'm sure he must have wanted to be there. Perhaps they simply felt that we couldn't afford to lose half a day's worth of his pay—they were always talking about how tight money was going to be when the baby came—or perhaps there was some other reason, I don't know, but he didn't even complain about not being able to go.

Davey worked at the same restaurant as Mom, in one of the big hotels downtown. That's how they met. Back when they had first started getting serious, Jack and I were pretty excited that our mother was dating an actual chef. We loved our mom but she was a terrible cook, she always overcooked everything. Every meal was either dried out if she baked it, soggy if she boiled it, or burnt if she tried to fry it.

So the idea of having a real chef in the family was pretty exciting, and at the time Jack even had a confused notion that black people can naturally cook better. "They have spices where he comes from," he said to me. Actually, he comes from St Vital, his family is from Trinidad but he was born here. We were disappointed, though. Even after he moved in, he didn't often cook for us. He said he had to cook meals for people every day at work, why would he want to spend his time off doing it at home? And when he *did* cook for us, usually when he'd had a few beers first, then he would often make it so spicy we could hardly eat it. He said they wouldn't let him put any kick in the food when he cooked at work, he had to make up for it at home, express himself a little. At least it made the house smell nice, even if we couldn't eat it.

The day of the ultrasound, Mom booked the whole day off from work. It was a beautiful warm morning, almost still like summer. The hospital was about a forty-minute walk from our house, but we left an hour and a half early and stopped halfway at a little Chinese beautician's Mom knew, where you could get a pedicure and manicure both for twenty-five bucks.

I'd never had either before. Mom purred like a cat when they were working over her feet, but I felt a little too embarrassed to really relax and enjoy it. And then the girl who was doing me kept asking if she could wax my eyebrows, and I didn't know how to feel about that, though Mom told me later that they always want to wax everybody's eyebrows, it had nothing to do with me personally. When the lady asked me what colour I wanted my nails painted, I wasn't sure, so she just picked a colour for me, a kind of eggplant colour, and I didn't have the courage to ask for something else. After they were finished with our toes, they made us sit for half an hour to let them dry. I tried to get up to go the washroom at one point and the lady got really angry.

We got to the hospital about ten or fifteen minutes before the appointment, and then we still had to wait for forty minutes on those uncomfortable plastic seats, in a room with five or six other pregnant ladies and their husbands or boyfriends or whatever.

"Do you think it's a girl?" I asked Mom again.

"I have no idea," she said, like she always did.

"But you hope it's a girl, right?"

"All I hope is it's healthy," she said, like she always did. I dismissed this as the sanctimonious sort of crap adults automatically hand you when they don't want to admit what they're really thinking. Deep down I suspected that she was hoping for another boy.

"Anyway," she added, "We'll find out soon enough."

"You know," I said, deciding to give it one last try, "You don't *have* to find out." I had looked into it—it was true. "Even if you get the ultrasound, if you say you don't want to know, they won't tell you." It was, I firmly believed, bad luck to learn the sex of the baby before it was born, sort of like peeking at your Christmas presents before they're wrapped, only even worse, cause Christmas comes every year but how often are you going to have a baby? There's nothing they can tell you that you won't find out eventually anyway. But she wouldn't listen to reason, and she said, "I bet you only think it's bad luck because Addy told you so," which I felt was a pretty hurtful and insulting thing to say, and also perfectly true although I wouldn't admit it.

"Sounds like an Addy idea to me," she said. "Anyway, if you think it's such bad luck, you don't have to know. Davey and Jack and I will all promise not to tell you."

Of course that would have been total torture for all of them to know and not me, I never could have stood it and Mom knew that too.

When the nurse came out and told Mom it was her turn, they wouldn't let me go in with her for the first part, and I had to wait another twenty or thirty minutes on my own before the nurse called my name and told me I could join them.

They took me to a little room where there were more machines and equipment than room for people to stand around. Mom was lying on her back on a gurney with her shirt up, a nurse was smearing her belly with some kind of clear jelly and running over it with a magic wand, and I looked in wonder at the elusive digital squiggle on the monitor that was my little sister-to-be, and at the blushing lovely face of my mother, smiling, shy, and almost crying. On the way home we stopped and had dim sum for lunch, Mom ate seven shrimp dumplings and I tried green tea for the first time.

After the ultrasound and we knew it was going to be a girl, I started putting a lot of thought into what name we needed to give her.

Addy and me, we had an argument about this. She said it was bad luck to pick the baby's name before she was born, you shouldn't even have a shortlist. You should wait until the baby comes out, get a good look at her, get to know her personality a bit and then figure out what name really fits her. After all, she said, just look what happened to her, getting stuck with a dead girl's name. But I felt just the opposite. I felt that picking the right name was the most important thing you could do, and that you ought to do it as early as possible, because the baby will grow to fit whatever name she's given, not the other way around.

So I bought a small blue notebook just for that, and the very first name I wrote down, one morning before breakfast, was Sally. A little sister named Sally, I felt certain, would be a little sister who would love me.

I can remember that morning so clearly. I was sitting at the kitchen table, with my feet up on a chair and the notebook propped on my knees, chewing the nail on my little finger and tapping the end of the pen against my leg like I always did when I was trying to concentrate.

Typhus was sitting on the table beside me, staring out the window, staring up at the family of sparrows that lived in our neighbour's eavestrough. Jack was over by the kitchen counter, making our sandwiches for lunch at school—cheese and mayonnaise on his, mustard and cucumber slices on mine, always the same, every day. He already had breakfast pretty much good to go. He had the hash browns and sausages in the oven and the eggs stirred up in a big glass bowl, ready for the frying pan.

Overhead we could hear Mom and Davey getting out of bed, the floorboards creaking as Mom hurried from the bedroom to the bathroom and back again—she always used to get out of bed and dressed in a rush in the mornings, all frantic as if she were running late for work, even if she had two or three hours before she had to leave—and then the sound of the shower turning on. Breakfast was the big meal in our home in those days, because during the week it was the only meal we could all eat together, sitting down like a family.

"What's a good middle name to go with Sally?" I said, thinking out loud. "Sally something, Sally what?"

My middle name is Thames, like the river in England, which is a stupid middle name and no one ever pronounces it right. Mom blames that name on Casey, she says Casey came up with the name in the hospital right after I was born, and Mom was still too whacked out from all the drugs to realize how dumb it was. And then by the time she came to her senses it was already too late, the forms were all filled out and official. Jack's middle name is Alexander, nothing wrong with that.

"Sally's a stupid name," Jack said. "That's a name for a doll, not a person."

I ignored him. I did actually have a doll named Sally when I was just a little kid, with a beanbag body and a fat plastic head and a puckered mouth to stick a toy bottle into, but that was years and years ago, and completely beside the point. "How about Sally Anne?" I asked, writing it down to see how it looked. Sally Anne Wellesley, Sally Anne Toussaint—I wasn't sure if Mom was going to give the baby our last name or Davey's. Then I tried writing it out again without the "e," like Sally Ann, to see which one looked better.

"Sally Ann?" said Jack. "You mean like the Salvation Army?"

"Hell," I said. I knew it had sounded familiar somehow. So I crossed it out and made a note.

"Sally Jane, maybe?" I said. "Sally Jean?"

"No, no," said Jack, making his voice and face completely serious. He poured the eggs into the frying pan, turned the heat on low, and put a cookie sheet over top to lid it. "I liked your first idea. We should name her Salvation Army, Salvation Army Wellesley, and then everyone can call her Sally Ann for short."

"Shut up," I said. "How about Sally Marie?"

Typhus suddenly leapt up at the window, arching his back and yowling frantically and scratching at the glass with his front paws, a hideous scraping screeching sound, and his big fat tail swept across the table, knocking over my glass of milk and it spilled right down my lap. He was just lucky it didn't get all over my notebook, and I swatted the stupid animal across the ass with it. He half-hissed, half-mewled at me, indignantly, and skittered clumsily off the table and out of the room.

Jack tossed me a towel, but I thought he should have had to clean it up since Typhus was his cat, so I just uprighted my empty glass and went to my room to change my pants.

When I got back, Jack's friend Conrad was sitting in Davey's spot, the wet towel was sitting in a lump on the table where I had left it, and there was milk on the seat of my chair and all over the floor. Conrad used to drop by in the mornings so we could all walk to school together, but sometimes he'd come extra-early so he could mooch breakfast off us if there was nothing good to eat at his house. He and Jack had been tight since grade three. They were in Tim Bits hockey together for half a year, and they got in a wrestling match after practice one time, out in the parking lot waiting to be picked up, and Jack accidentally dislocated Conrad's ankle when he pushed him backwards while standing on his foot. Conrad had to wear a cast for four weeks, and they were best friends ever since. I liked him because he was so skinny and he wore those nerdy glasses, and because he and his family lived with his grandma who called him Connie and he didn't try to make her stop even though he cringed every time she said it. Because like he told me once, shrugging helplessly, "She's my Nana, I can't tell her what to call me."

Typhus was sitting on the table, lapping happily at the pool of spilled milk, and Conrad was saying, "Sally? Wasn't that her dolly's name?"

"Shut up," I said, sitting down in Jack's seat. "How did you know that?" Jack must have told him to say that, I'm sure that I stopped playing with that doll long before Conrad was ever around.

"Natalie," said Mom angrily, coming into the kitchen just at that moment, "you don't tell people to 'shut up' in my house. And take your feet off the chair, how many times do I have to tell you that?"

"Sorry, Mom."

Davey, coming in behind her, said, "What is that cat doing on our table? How many times have I told you not to let that cat up on the table?"

Jack said, "Natalie thinks we should name the baby Sally."

"Is that milk? Who spilled that milk? Why is no one cleaning up that milk?" said Davey angrily.

"Sally?" said Mom. "Wasn't that the name of your old dolly?"

"You're all just gonna sit there and look at the spilled milk? Is no one going to clean up that milk? What's wrong with you people?"

"I hated that doll," said Mom. "It smelled like pee and you screamed every time I tried to put the stupid thing through the wash."

Davey wanted to name the baby after his great-aunt, Tante Martìne, who raised him from when he was just a little kid, but that wasn't going to happen. The truth was that none of us could stand Tante Martìne and I don't think she liked us much either, though we all sucked it up and tried to get along for Davey's sake.

She was a tiny tough shrivelled old woman who smelled like a burnt match in the bathroom and walked with a cane. I don't think she really needed it to help her walk, she just liked having it to whack things with. She once asked Mom if she drank a lot when she was pregnant with me, and she used to ask all kinds of ridiculous questions about me and Jack's father, bringing him up in conversation all the time until even Davey put his foot down about it.

When Mom first got pregnant and they were still talking about we'd need to move to a bigger place, Davey wanted to borrow the money from Tante Martìne so that we could buy a house instead of having to rent. But if they did that, they'd have to invite her to come live with us as well, and then what if she said yes? She was living in a seniors' complex at the time, out in St Vital. And even though I know Mom would have loved to own her own home, it had been a dream of hers for years, there was just no way she was willing to pay that price. And no way in hell was she going to name the baby Martìne.

If Davey couldn't have Martìne, he wanted a long, exotic kind of name like Nicoletta, or Evangelina, or Mercedes. I remember he even suggested Argentina, which isn't really a name at all. I wanted a shorter, more old-fashioned sounding name, like Ellen or Alice, if I couldn't have Sally.

Jack kept suggesting boys' names, like Alex or Corey or Henry. "I think a girl named Henry would be really cool," he said, and I said, "You mean like Henrietta?" and he said, "No, just Henry."

Mom was my biggest disappointment. After all, I thought Jack and Natalie were pretty decent names and she had chosen those. I felt sure she'd be on my side. But I could never get her to make any suggestions at all. All she would do is reject every name that anyone else would come up with, no matter what. She wouldn't even give a maybe or "I'll think about it", it was always, "No way, not a chance," or "Over my dead body." Which made me suspect that she had already settled on a name she knew the rest of us would hate, and didn't want to tell us until it was too late to argue.

I took all kinds of baby-name books out of the library and collected lists of suggestions from everybody we knew, I used to read them out to her thinking that if I happened to say the name she'd secretly picked I would see it in her face, but all she would do is get irritable and say, "She's my daughter and I'll name her whatever I want. End of conversation."

# 8

EMMANUEL STUMBLED, AND HAVING STUMBLED, HE DROPPED first to his knees and then flopped down onto his face. He took care, Rose noticed, not to hurt himself, while still trying to give the impression of dropping heavily. And then he lay there motionless, face down on the dusty street, and said, in a voice humming and rich with self-pity, "Go on without me."

The first time he had done something like this, Rose had been deeply concerned; the second time, she was exasperated, even angry; but now, she found she was really just amused, and looked down at him with a certain fondness. "Okay," she said.

He shifted slightly where he lay but didn't lift his head, and he said, "I'm serious, I mean it. Go on without me, you're better off without me. Go find your sister."

"Okay," Rose said again, in a deliberately cheerful and careless voice. And she started to walk away. She walked slowly, strolling casually, not turning her head to look back but listening, hoping to hear him scrabbling to his feet and following her. But she wanted to be careful not to go too fast or too far, lest they inadvertently get separated by the shifting and treacherous streets. She wasn't ready to get separated from him; she had grown used to having him around. After she'd walked only a couple dozen yards she stopped, looked back to where he still lay, motionless, and shook her head. Then she lowered herself carefully onto the stoop of the nearest building. Out of the corner of her eye she could see him lift his head to look at her, and then quickly lower it again.

Rose took the coil of rope and laid it on the stoop beside her, rubbing her shoulder where it had started to chafe. Then she began massaging her stiff and aching calves. She was desperately tempted to take off her boots and do the same for her feet, which were cramping and blistered and frostbitten, but she was too afraid to take even the slightest chance of getting separated from them. There was no one in the street with them right now, but someone could appear at any moment. And in the week or two that they had been travelling together—impossible to tell how long it had been really—she had seen how much Emmanuel suffered from having bare feet. The further they ventured into the city, the rougher the streets were becoming, busted up with cracks and potholes, strewn with rubble and sharp rocks, thistles and splinters of wood, shards of glass and puddles of blood.

Looking around, wondering how long he would just lie there, and if she was going to have to go back and cajole him, Rose noticed that there was something strange about the door of the building across the street. There was something carved into the wood. Frowning, she collected the rope and got to her feet and crossed over to take a closer look. "Emmanuel," she called out. "Emmanuel, come see this."

In crude and deep-cut letters an inch and a half high, someone had carved the words, *The Queen will set you free.*

Rose ran her fingers gently over the inscription, shuddering slightly, she wasn't sure why. Emmanuel had come and joined her, standing just behind her and looking past her at the inscription.

"The queen," she said. "What is the queen, what do you think it means?"

"I don't know," he replied. "I've seen it before, though."

"Yeah, me too." She told him about the courtyard she had come across, and what was written on the walls in blood. And he told Rose about a woman who had accosted him once, and asked him, with a kind of feverish excitement, if he was "going to see the queen." This woman had been so skinny that he could see each articulated bone in her face and arms and legs, straining against her taut and yellow skin. She was so skeletal he imagined he could hear her bones clacking as she approached him. When she spoke about the queen she had smiled, a wide, ghastly, almost beatific smile, and reached out a claw-like hand to caress him, and he had turned in a panic and ran. This had happened when he was still newly dead, and hadn't yet fully comprehended just where he was. Emmanuel had already told Rose the story of how he died, by jumping from the side of a boat and drowning. It was on the ferry to Catalina Island with his whole class on board, and it hadn't been a planned or calculated death, though he said he'd often had moods or moments before when he'd wished he were dead, like black wings beating in his face.

That's all it had taken, just a single and suddenly overwhelming impulse of shame and humiliation that passed almost before he was in the cold hard water, hitting the waves with an impact that knocked the breath out of him and almost knocked him senseless. He could still remember the stinging in his eyes and the burning sensation in his nose and throat as the salty water rushed in, the distorted cries of alarm from the boat as the waves tossed him back and forth, the expectation of being rescued and the sense of humiliation that that, too, would entail. And then he was under the water, and it was just the excruciatingly long slow death of drowning that he could still recall every unbearable second of. He seemed even now, after all this time, to hardly believe that a single impulsive leap, a fleeting moment of self-hatred, almost instantly regretted, could have been so final, complete and irreparable.

They talked a lot, Rose and Emmanuel, about their lives; there wasn't much else to talk about. He'd told her about his life in California, how his parents were both doctors, wealthy and important and hardly ever home. His mother worked in the emergency room of a large hospital and his father was a plastic surgeon, they lived in a sprawling ugly house just outside of Anaheim, with three grapefruit trees and an Olympic-sized swimming pool in the backyard. But the swimming pool never had any water in it, because his mother had once had to pronounce dead a four-year-old boy who had drowned in a swimming pool just like it. She told Emmanuel that they would put water in the pool once he had learned to swim, but whenever he had asked her to sign him up for swimming lessons she always put him off, said things were too busy, I don't think you're ready yet, maybe next year, baby. And he had told Rose how once he had climbed down into the empty pool to play, this was when he was nine, but he couldn't get back out again. He could just graze the bottom rung of the ladder with his fingertips when he jumped, and he had to yell for almost an hour before the housekeeper found him, but instead of helping him out the housekeeper had just left him down there until his father came home.

    His father wouldn't help him out either. Instead he lowered down a peanut butter sandwich and two bananas, a bottle of apple juice, a sleeping bag and a bucket to pee in, and told him he would have to spend the whole night down there and think about what he had done, why he ought to be more careful in the future, listen to his parents and not play in places he knew he wasn't supposed to go. They didn't really make him spend the night, though, only four or five more hours until after it got dark; then his father came back out and shone a flashlight down on his face and asked him if he had learned his lesson. His mother wasn't home at the time—she was doing a double-shift at the hospital. She often wasn't home.

    Rose had told him how she died, too, but mostly she talked about Bethany. It was better than thinking about herself, and she was determined to keep her spirits up; keep her hopes up.

    "You'll love her, I know it," she said to Emmanuel. "Everybody loves her, she's so beautiful."

    There was a caustic, rueful undertone to her voice, but Emmanuel didn't seem to notice it. "She must look like you, then," he said, meeting her eyes briefly and then quickly looking away again, at the ground, blushing bright red.

    She realized later that the poor kid must have meant it as a bold and gallant compliment, perhaps even a shy declaration of puppy love, but in the moment, it only brought back to Rose the bitterest and most painful of her memories from the last few months of her life, and how sometimes her father would drunkenly call her

"Bethany" when he'd steal into her room, and those were memories she didn't ever, ever want to think about for even a moment. "Don't worry," Emmanuel said abruptly. "We'll find her, I promise. I'll help you find her." After a moment's thought—perhaps thinking, as she was, about how little he could actually *do* to help, however sincerely he intended what he said—he added, "I can speak a bit of Spanish, you know."

And so the very next person they saw, Emmanuel eagerly called out to him from a distance, yelling, "*Hola! Hola! Puede usted ayudarnos?*"

The man had his back to them, squatting down in the middle of the street. He had no shirt on. As they got nearer, they could see a starburst of light brown scars against his dark brown skin, and a rivulet of blood trickling down from the back of his head and along his spine. He was wearing ragged canvas pants, tied around the waist with a pair of shoelaces, and rubber sandals on his feet. He had a scarred-over stump where his right arm ought to have been.

Emmanuel repeated his question as they got closer, and the man said, "*Désolé?*" as he turned around, making a gesture of irritated incomprehension. He had a bullet hole instead of his left eye, and Rose caught a glimpse of the white and jagged bone of his eye socket, poking out from the pulp and pulsing blood. He had a scrap of jagged metal in his one hand, he'd been scraping and digging at the hard dirt road for some reason she never understood—he must have been working at it for some time, for he had scraped out a hole a foot wide and perhaps half a foot deep so far, puddled with the blood that was pouring from his eye socket.

Rose knew a little French, from school—indeed, she found she could remember more of what she had learned in class now than she ever could in life, just as she could remember everything about her life so clearly here. She knew her pronunciation must be pretty bad, and her vocabulary was rudimentary, but though he appeared to understand *her*, she could make little sense of his rapid and slang-filled responses. He seemed to be asking them for something, but she couldn't make out what. It must have had something to do with the hole he was digging, for he began gesturing at it in an agitated way, talking faster and more forcibly than ever.

When Rose tried to speak of "*ma soeur*," he cut her off angrily, spitting out the words "*Merci mingi*," with a tone of bitter sarcasm, and turned his back on them, squatting down again and returning to his digging and scraping, ignoring her further attempts to communicate.

Turning to the right at the next intersection, they found themselves on a spacious street that sloped gradually downwards. The houses on either side of them were bewildering and ornate monstrosities, three and sometimes four storeys high, with towers and turrets and cupolas, gables and eaves carved with hearts and flowers, wrap-around porches with sagging roofs and broken pillars, balconies tumbled down or hanging precariously by a few boards, all painted in flaking and dirty shades of pink and yellow and powder blue. The houses were set well above them on the hillside, and made unreachable by a wild and tangled overgrowth of black and thorny hedges, purple loosestrife, clinging vines and gnarled forbidding trees that in some places grew right through the porches, heaving up through the splintered wood, or extending their thick boughs through the shattered bay windows.

The street began to slope down more steeply as they walked; the curbs grew higher and higher until they became walls and the houses disappeared out of sight, with only an occasional spire or crumbling chimney visible, rising above the trees. They were approaching an underpass now, a tunnel beneath a street that looked so thin, like a bare sliver of concrete. It hardly looked as if it would support the weight of a single person walking over it, let alone the row of houses that lined it, perched precariously at the very edge and looking as if they might topple over backwards at any moment.

"I don't like this," said Rose. "I think we should turn around."

And they did, but somehow the slope of the street turned with them, and the underpass was there in front of them again. They tried turning again, and again they were going down. The concrete walls on either side of them were fifteen feet high now, sheer and unbroken, the slope of the street some twenty-five or thirty degrees down to the mouth of the underpass, where it appeared to level out at last.

"I guess we don't have a choice," Rose said. "I guess we're going under."

"I guess so," said Emmanuel.

When they entered the tunnel they could see the opening at the far side quite plainly, and the street sloping back upwards on the other side. It looked to be no further than thirty or forty yards away. But the further they walked towards it, the further away it receded. Above them, thick and twisted tree roots snaked down from the ceiling, in some places reaching low enough to almost graze their heads. Drops of blood fell slowly, rhythmically from the tapered ends of the roots, landing in dull splashes that echoed unnervingly. The drops of blood had formed a pool that covered the uneven ground, in some places so deep that it threatened the tops of Rose's boots, seeping in over the tongues. Emmanuel, with his bare feet and ankles, could feel that the thick and disgustingly warm blood was actually flowing gently ahead of them, meaning that even though they appeared to be on level ground, they were actually going downhill still. "Let's go back," he said. "I don't like this, I don't like this at all."

"I don't like it either," said Rose. "But if we try going back, it'll probably only get worse." But she quietly slipped her hand in his. It was clammy and soft, and he squeezed gently and hung on.

They walked for several minutes without seeming to make any progress. Looking behind them, the entrance from the street was no longer visible, the tunnel stretching on into the darkness in both directions, as far as the eye could see. Then a little further on, and there were no more tree roots hanging above their heads, the echoey drip-drip-drip of blood was replaced by a sound like melting snow going down a storm drain, and the wind stopped completely. The ceiling was getting lower and the walls were getting closer, though still wide enough for them to walk side by side. The slope of the ground grew steeper again, so that Emmanuel almost lost his footing, and had to hold on to Rose's shoulder to steady himself on the slimy, smooth and slippery ground. The pool of blood was growing deeper and deeper—above the tops of Rose's boots, above her calves, up to her knees, above her knees. She had to gather the skirt of her dress and hold it up at her waist, hoping to keep it mostly dry. Emmanuel did the same with the jacket, and they waded steadily forward.

The blood that to Emmanuel felt unpleasantly warm, as if it were spilled directly fresh from a living body, felt almost hot against Rose's frozen and frostbitten skin. She knew that feeling from when she was alive. She was reminded of times in winter when she would come in from playing outside in the cold and snow, and run her hands under the tap, and then even cold water would feel uncomfortably warm at first, and her fingers would throb and scream with pain until they had finished thawing out. Only here she would never thaw out, and the pain would never subside.

One moment the end of the tunnel appeared as far away from them as it ever had. A few more steps and it was suddenly in front of them: a broken open window, set in a red and crumbling brick wall, with the blood lapping and spilling over the edge of the window sill onto the platform of a fire escape, five storeys above the street.

It was such a relief to come out of the tunnel at last, that even feeling the wind buffeting against them was a kind of pleasure, and they collapsed in a heap in the corner of the fire escape. Rose began to cry, a mixture of pain and relief, as Emmanuel tried awkwardly to comfort her, using the sleeves of his jacket to wipe the blood from her legs.

She tried to take off her boots, but she couldn't get any grip on the blood-soaked laces with her stiff and aching fingers, and had to ask Emmanuel to do it for her. It took him a long time, but when he had them undone and pulled them off at last, he helped her peel the soaking wet socks from her feet—warm to his touch, hot to hers—and threw them from the fire escape down to the alley below. Emmanuel wiped the blood from her feet and toes, and he even tried his best to soak up the blood from the inside of her boots as Rose wiped the tears and the snot from her face, now laughing weakly. Then looking up, she saw that someone was watching them. It was a man, standing on the roof of the building above them. He had sparse and sandy hair that blew limply in the wind, his cheeks were pocked and pitted, and he wore a pair of square glasses, the frame slightly bent so that they sat askew on his face. He was leaning over the busted parapet, watching them with an unpleasant grin. He winked at Rose when she looked up at him, and called out to her, with a slight accent that wasn't quite German, saying, "Why don't you come up and play?" Then there was a noise, coming from the roof behind him, the sound of something crashing and an excited commotion of voices, and he disappeared from sight.

Rose and Emmanuel were on the top platform of the fire escape, perhaps ten or twelve feet below the roof; a metal ladder reached up. Emmanuel tried calling out to the man, but he didn't return.

"What do you think?" he asked Rose.

"Help me put my boots back on," was all she said. When he had them laced up for her, she walked over to the ladder, gave it a shake to see if it would hold, and then started carefully up, pausing occasionally to wipe the palm of her left hand where the blood made it slippery.

Up on the rooftop, Rose and Emmanuel could see for miles, but all that they could see was more of the same: a whole city of red brick buildings, four and five storeys high, stretching out in close rows in every direction. The wind swirled and curled and eddied, skittering pebbles and chips of bricks across the concrete.

In many places the parapet had been pulled half down or more, to make use of the bricks. Near the middle of the roof, a half-dozen people were gathered in a loose circle, the sandy-haired man with the glasses among them. He wore a brown tweed suit and had his hands in his pants pockets, where he jiggled them restlessly.

Several of the people glanced over at Rose and Emmanuel as they neared, but showed little interest. Only the man with the glasses acknowledged them, taking his right hand out of his pocket to wave hello and then putting a finger to his lips to indicate quiet. Rose noticed that his glasses had a lens on the right side only, and on the left was just an empty frame. He winked, put his hand back in his pocket, and turned his attention back to the game.

Two men and a small, slender woman with rag-bound wrists were squatting around a pile of bricks in the middle of the circle, slowly building a precarious tower. Each took a turn to add a single brick, sometimes laying it flat, sometimes on one side or even up on end; sometimes straight, sometimes at an angle. The object seemed to be to make certain you didn't topple any bricks yourself, while making it as difficult as possible for the next player to do the same. They played slowly and deliberately, sometimes studying the tower for a minute or more before taking their turn.

Everyone watched the game intently, now and then exchanging glances or making discreet gestures to one another. There was a middle-aged woman with a bleary face, who wore a blue and flowered nightgown and a brown fedora and who seemed to struggle to stay awake, often yawning and rubbing her eyes; Rose wondered if she had died by taking sleeping pills. At one point, her eyelids fell shut for as much as a minute, and she swayed on her feet as precariously as the tower of bricks, until the man beside her gently held her elbow and the small of her back to steady her, and her eyes fluttered open again.

He was an elderly man, the man at her side, with great flapping ears and a head that was much too large for his body. He was completely bald, except for thick bristles of white hair protruding from his ears and nostrils, and his head was covered with deep brown spots. Like the man with the glasses, he wore an old-fashioned brown suit with red suspenders and a red bow tie, dirty and limp, also incongruous white sneakers that must surely have belonged to someone else. On the other side of the woman was a wiry brown man with a bloody rag tied around his throat, and bright black eyes, nervous as a bird, who often paced away from the circle between plays. He would rub his hands energetically in front of his face when a brick was being placed.

The tower had been about two feet high when Rose and Emmanuel joined the circle. It was close to five feet high when one of the players, a flabby man with heavily lidded eyes and blue lips under a thick and tangled beard, mislaid his brick and brought it toppling down. Everyone jumped back a foot or two, with a roar of excitement, when it fell; the man with the glasses had to skip smartly out of the way to avoid one brick coming down heavily on his bare foot.

Several people cheered, and the woman with the slashed wrists laughed and clapped her hands, while the fat man who had toppled the tower walked a little ways off, complaining loudly, and no one paid any attention to him. The spectators, free to talk now, were chatting animatedly to one another in several languages. The black-eyed man was jabbering in Spanish, too fast for Emmanuel to catch more than a couple words. He had taken a penknife out of his pocket, with a tortoiseshell clasp and a nicked and tarnished blade about an inch and a half long, and handed it over to the little old man with the flapping ears, who accepted it with a very small bow and a very wide smile, showing no teeth. The man with the glasses called out to him, pointing at the knife and asking a question. The little old man grinned again but shook his head, making a *tut-tut-tut* sound.

The only person who showed no particular emotion was the third player, a stolid looking man with a square-cut moustache and a wrinkled and congested face. He had the broad and thickly calloused hands of a labourer and the braided and livid red throat of a hanged man. He and the woman with the slashed wrists began patiently, methodically clearing the tower of bricks, tossing any broken ones into a pile far off on the side.

As they cleared the bricks, the man with glasses turned his attention to Rose now, first saying, "English, yes?"

Rose nodded, and the man said, "Who do you think will win, hey?" gesturing at the two players, who were now laying out a bottom row of bricks, three by three, to build the next tower on.

"The woman," said Rose, who liked the look of her plain and thoughtful face. And then, too, the woman's slit wrists reminded Rose of Malcolm, who had been so kind to her. The woman heard what Rose said, and glanced up at her with a quick shy smile.

"And you, hey?" said the man, speaking to Emmanuel now.

"The woman," said Emmanuel firmly.

"You want to bet, yes?" said the man, his grey eyes gleaming. "My jacket," he offered, looking over at Emmanuel, whose own jacket was now torn at the shoulder and soaked with blood. "My jacket, your boots," he said to Rose.

"No," said Emmanuel, before Rose could answer. "Not her boots." But the man ignored him, still looking at Rose; everyone was looking at them, even the players, who had finished getting the game ready and were waiting to begin. Rose shook her head no.

"The rope, then," said the man. "The rope for my jacket."

Rose hesitated, and Emmanuel spoke up, saying loudly, almost defiantly, "We're looking for her sister." He described Bethany, the way Rose had described her to him. "Has anyone here seen her, seen a girl like that?"

"No, no," said the man with the glasses, with little interest. The gleam in his eyes had gone out. The others murmured no as well, some with sympathy, some with impatience or disinterest. And then a voice came from behind them, saying, "I met a girl here who looked like you."

Rose turned around; it was the man who had toppled the tower and lost the game, and he was looking her over with interest from beneath his heavy eyelids. "You give me that rope, I'll tell you all about her."

"Don't be an asshole," said the woman in the circle, but the man said, "Mind your own business, Margaret," without ever removing his gaze from Rose's face. He held his hands out with the palms up and fingers spread.

"She looked very much like you, very pretty girl," said the man. "She must have been your sister—I never heard her name. I can even tell you how to look for her."

Rose was torn between wanting to hope, and the fear of being disappointed. She asked him to describe what Bethany was wearing. It was the same clothes she had on when she had died. Rose slipped the rope from her shoulder and tossed it to the ground at the man's feet. "When did you see her?" she asked. "How long ago?"

He shrugged. "A month, two months ago, I don't know."

"Did you talk to her? Where did you see her, what was she doing?"

"She was with a group of people, three, four people. They were doing the pilgrim thing."

"I don't understand."

"They were pilgrims," he said. "True believers. They were trying to find the queen."

# 9

WHEN I HAD CALLED ADDY TO TELL HER ABOUT THE ULTRASOUND, and how I was going to have a little sister, she had been disappointed that it wasn't twins.

"Maybe one of them was just hiding behind the other one and you couldn't see her."

"Yeah," I said doubtfully. "There's not *that* much room in there, you know, I think they would have noticed that."

"I guess," she said. "Oh well, that's ten bucks down the drain." And she made a little *poof*ing noise. She'd made a bet on it with her mom, she told me.

"Maybe you could lie about it?" I suggested.

"No," said Addy—I thought just a little bit reluctantly. "It's definitely bad luck to lie about a bet. Besides, Mom would call and check, she and Nora don't talk that often but they do talk."

I thought this was really bad news, because Addy was supposed to be saving up money for a ticket to Winnipeg, and ten bucks is ten bucks.

Like we had expected, when Addy had asked her if she could come to Winnipeg for Christmas, Casey had said something like, "I'd love to get rid of you for two weeks, but we can't afford that." And Addy had said, "What if I pay half, and the other half could be my Christmas gift?" and Casey said, "Sure, fine, whatever." Not, you know, thinking she'd have to make good on it, because Addy couldn't ever put her hands on five bucks, let alone a few hundred.

I had thirty-four bucks in the bank that I immediately sent her as my share, but I couldn't get Mom or Jack to contribute, and Davey when I asked him just looked at me like I was talking in

Japanese or Sanskrit or something, and changed the subject. So that left about two hundred and sixty-six bucks to make up, only she had to make it up in the next two or three months, because the prices go up if you don't buy your tickets way ahead of time. And Casey had said no way in hell to Addy taking the Greyhound by herself, which I think she would have actually preferred, cause like she said, you'd probably meet some pretty interesting people.

So this was Addy's first idea to raise the money: Casey had an old guitar that just sat in a corner of the apartment anyway, she only brought it out once in a blue moon when she had people over and she was drunk enough. So when she'd go to work in the mornings —this was still in the summer, before school started—Addy would haul it out and try to teach herself to play. She got a beginner's book out from the library, and she told me she was amazed at how quickly she picked it up. "I must be a prodigy or something," she said. She tried playing me something over the phone. It sounded pretty awful, honestly, but maybe the phone line distorted it a bit, like she said.

Anyway, after a week or two of practising, she figured she was good to go, and when her mom left for work, Addy packed a bag lunch and headed out to busk on Atwater.

The first day she made four dollars and seventy-two cents for six hours work. She blamed it on the location, so the next day she went a little further afield, up to Georges Vanier Station, where she got eleven dollars, twelve cents, and two sexual propositions: "Two serious ones, anyway." On the third day she was only out there for less than an hour when one of her mom's co-workers spotted her, and that put an end to that. She'd made a buck forty that morning before she got busted, so that was a grand total of seventeen dollars and twenty-four cents and only two hundred and forty-eight seventy-six left to go, as long as Casey came through with the other half like she said she would.

But now, if she'd lost ten in that bet to Casey about it being twins, that set her back to just over forty bucks, which is why I was so disappointed.

"Hey, it's just a bet," she said. "If you can't take it like a man, you shouldn't gamble in the first place," she added, a little pompously, as if I'd been the one making bad bets and she was lecturing me about it.

"But if you can't buy those tickets soon…" I started to say.

"Oh, that? Didn't I tell you? Mom already bought the tickets for me. She put it on her credit card, we're all good to go."

Addy, it turned out, had gone down a few days before—it had been a few days since I had talked to her—and sold her hair, her beautiful long red hair, to a fancy salon. "They gave me a hundred bucks for it," she said. "I couldn't believe it, a hundred bucks!" She had to give twenty to the lady she'd paid to pretend to be her mother and give her permission, but even so, that was eighty bucks straight profit for maybe ten minutes work.

Casey completely freaked out, of course, even worse than with the busking thing. Addy didn't really go into that too much, but it sounded like there was a lot of screaming and some broken dishes, shit like that, and then the next day Casey booked the flight. Maybe she was feeling a little guilty about flipping out so bad, though of course she wouldn't have admitted it. She just said to Addy, "Here, before you go and whore yourself out on the street, you little freak."

"And the best part," Addy told me triumphantly, "Is that she only made me give her a hundred dollars, so I'm up thirty bucks. Well, twenty now, I guess."

My mom and Casey had grown up in the country together, this was about an hour northwest of the city, went to school together, hung out all the time. They were best friends growing up, just like sisters, just like Addy and me. When they were eighteen, they had moved to the city together to go to university. They shared a little apartment just off campus, but Mom says they didn't go to classes very much. She always told me and Jack that we should wait to go to university until we're, like, twenty-five at least, cause when you're eighteen or nineteen you're too dumb, drunk and horny to really get the most out of it anyway, she'd say.

Anyway, that spring, after classes were over, they got hired on with a tree-planting crew to spend the summer working in Northern Ontario. They both got hired on, cause they did everything together, but then Mom found out she was pregnant with Jack and had to drop out, cause she didn't know if that kind of strenuous work could hurt the baby, and what if anything happened? They'd be so far away from a hospital or even any doctors. So Casey went alone, and she must have got pregnant up north some time after she got out there, but she never ever said how it happened or with who the father was—not to Mom, not to Addy, not to anyone, ever.

Casey's such a small person and so fragile-looking I can't imagine her doing that kind of work, which it's supposed to be pretty intense and a lot of digging and heavy lifting, but she must have done a good job cause they hired her again the next summer, and all the summers after that. She went and did it every year until Addy was seven or eight, all over the country—northern Ontario, Quebec, even out in northern BC—and Addy would come stay with us for the couple months that Casey would be away planting, since she and Jack were like brother and sister anyway.

From the time she first got pregnant, pretty much right up until she gave birth, Casey was possessed by this constant need to be moving around. She said it wasn't too bad at first, when she was up north, because she was on her feet working all day anyway; and of course she didn't realize that she was pregnant yet. She said she'd go for a walk first thing in the morning while everyone else was still eating breakfast, and then in the evenings after dinner she'd go for a walk again. Just short little walks at first, but they gradually got longer and longer, even though her feet would be blistered and her legs and back aching, she just had to keep moving, she couldn't seem to help herself somehow.

She told herself that it was just because she loved the wilderness so much, and the solitude, it was so beautiful up there. She was always talking about how beautiful it was up there. One night near the end of the season she walked too far and got lost. The sun went down and she stumbled around for hours until she found a service road, and her supervisor sent her home after that, for her own safety.

By then she knew that she was pregnant too. She dropped out of university, just like Mom, but she couldn't bear the thought of moving back home. My father had moved into the apartment with Mom while Casey was gone, so now the three of them were living together in this tiny little place and Casey with the walking sickness worse than ever.

At first she really tried to hide it—you know, make it seem normal, like she was just trying to stay in shape and pass the time. She'd make Mom go for walks around the neighbourhood with her, since neither of them had jobs or anything else to do anyway. If she was stuck in the apartment she'd constantly be sweeping and cleaning and stuff, which doesn't sound like Casey at all, but it was really just so she'd have an excuse to be up and moving about, and her feet got wicked blisters after a while, and the veins in her legs started popping out of her skin.

Mom says that Casey even started walking in her sleep after a while, and everyone was worried about her, especially as she got more and more pregnant—Casey being so petite, and with twins inside her she got absolutely huge. By the end her belly was bigger than the rest of her put together. Her hips were practically dislocated and her legs couldn't support the weight any more, they were ready to snap like twigs underneath her.

She had to spend the last few weeks in bed. The only time they let her get up was to go to the toilet, and they made her use a walker just to do that. Apparently at night you could see her legs moving under the covers the whole time she was asleep, moving steadily up and down as if she was walking in her dreams. And Casey made them buy her all kinds of maps, books of maps of this city and cities all around the world, and she'd lay there in bed, totally immobile, staring at the maps all day long and taking imaginary walks inside their lines.

When Mom went into labour, about two weeks late, then Casey went into labour with her, and even though she was two months early the babies were just as big as Jack. They had to give Casey a C-section; they say that Addy came out with her eyes wide open already, looking around and checking things out, which isn't normal at all. But Maddy had the umbilical cord wrapped around her little throat. She was already dead, and the doctors said she'd probably been dead for hours and hours, probably from not long after Casey's labour began.

Addy says her grandmother once took her to see Maddy's grave, she has a distant but very definite memory of it. She must have been just three years old, because her grandfather passed away a few months before she turned four, and she never saw her grandma again after that. Her grandpa wasn't with them that day, it was just the two of them, and she remembers driving in to the city, she remembers the tall black cemetery gates with crabapple trees along the walls, a cool, grey day and a small, clean headstone. But when she asked her mother about it once, years later, Casey said she must have made the whole thing up, or dreamed it or something; she said that there was no grave, that Maddy was never buried at all, they had her cremated and scattered the ashes along the banks of the river.

Addy lived with her grandparents out in the country until she was almost four. Sometimes she'd live with her mother, for a month here, or a month there, but mostly with her grandparents. Casey moved around a lot, even then. For as long as I could remember, Casey had always been going away, sometimes for a month or two, sometimes for forever, which "forever" generally ended up being half a year or a year and a half before she came back. Sometimes she took Addy with her, sometimes she left her behind.

Addy's grandparents had a farm, what they call a PMU farm, a pregnant-mare's-urine farm. It's where they take the piss out of pregnant horses and sell it to make birth control pills. Her grandma was a tiny woman who used to pinch Addy on the underside of her arm when she was being bad, hard enough to leave a mark. Addy remembers her always smelling like freshly mowed grass, even in the winter, and she wore her red and grey hair in a braid that hung down past the small of her back. She promised Addy she'd teach her how to braid it some day, but then she never did.

Addy's grandpa was fat and clumsy and kind, he wore tinted yellow glasses and hardly ever talked. He used to sneak candy behind his wife's back, he especially loved anything fruit-flavoured, like lollipops and gummi bears and those little coloured marshmallows. He used to hide little stashes of them in his toolbox, or out in the barn, or behind the books on the bookshelf, and sometimes he'd let Addy share some with him when her grandmother wasn't around. Then he'd go and smoke a cigarette so his wife wouldn't smell the candy on his breath when she came home and she kissed him.

Her grandpa died in the fall, from a heart attack or stroke or something. It was pretty sudden—it wasn't like he was sick or anything—and he was only fifty, which I guess that's pretty young if you're talking about actually dying. His wife had left him watching a baseball game when she went to bed and she said he seemed perfectly fine. Addy was the one who found him the next morning, cold on the bathroom floor with his pants around his ankles and his lucky ball cap on and some half-chewed jellybeans falling out of his open mouth. The funny thing was that he also had these two huge bruises on his back, purple and black fat bruises in the shape of horseshoes, but no one knew anything about him being kicked or where those bruises might have come from. This was the same year the Expos won the World Series.

Casey and her mother had a big fight after the funeral, Addy can remember hearing them yell at each other in the kitchen when she was supposed to be asleep in bed, and she went to live with her mother from then on. Mostly her mother and sometimes us. Addy's grandma sold the farm, and with all that money she bought an RV. She said she'd spent her whole life never going more than a hundred miles from the spot she was born, and she had always promised herself that one day, when all her work was done, she was going to take a look around. She spent the rest of her life travelling across North America and sending in fake notices of her death to newspapers everywhere she went.

According to some of the obituaries she wrote about herself, she studied gourmet cooking in Orlando, was the first female jockey to ever compete in the Breeders' Cup at Belmont, served as a translator for the American military during the Vietnam War, suffered from several rare diseases, spent time in a Rhode Island prison after being convicted of stealing, killing and eating a purebred King Charles spaniel, was abducted and vivisected by black-market organ thieves in El Centro, California, drowned off the coast of northern BC on a whale-watching expedition, and died of multiple stab wounds while working to reclaim child prostitutes from the streets of Denver, Colorado. Those are just the ones I remember. She used to mail the clippings from the obituary sections to Casey when they came out. At least we all figured it was her, there was never any name on the envelope or letter or anything along with them.

When Addy was in grade six, she disappeared one day from a school field trip and didn't turn up until almost ten o'clock at night, her shoes all caked with mud, her nose crusted with blood, and her long red hair all tangled with twigs and burrs and dry brown leaves. I think this was late September or early October.

I remember being in school that day, and how the rumours started spreading that something had gone seriously wrong on the grade six field trip. The first story that went around, over lunch, was that the bus had broken down and they were stuck out in the middle of nowhere. By afternoon recess, I heard the bus had been sideswiped by a pick-up truck that ran a red light, and half the kids were in the hospital. Three o'clock came and went and the bus didn't come back as scheduled, and then three-thirty came and went, the bell rang, and school was out and the bus still hadn't come back. Even more kids than usual hung around the schoolyard after classes instead of going home. I didn't really have a choice but to hang around, I had to wait for Jack to walk me home—he had the key to our apartment.

The bus finally arrived at about quarter past four. To my imagination, there was something shabby and defeated about the way it pulled up along the side street, and in the sad long exhale as it opened its doors. The kids and teachers filed off, looking tired, tense, angry and afraid. Jack was one of the last to get off, and he looked absolutely furious. And then, of course, Addy didn't get off at all.

One of the teachers told Jack to come to the office with him, but Jack didn't even bother to look back, he just said, "I have to take my little sister home," and put his arm around my shoulder and started to walk me away. He didn't actually flip the teacher the middle finger, but you felt like he might as well have. As we walked away I snuck a peek behind us. That teacher was just standing there glaring at Jack with a look of absolute loathing, all baffled and beet red. It was Mr. Benson, with the big chunky moon face and the flat grey hair that sat at kind of a weird angle on his head, the one who always wore those sweaters.

Apparently right before she disappeared, Addy had whispered something to Jack like, "Cover for me, I'll be right back." This was about midway through the morning, maybe forty-five minutes or an hour before lunch, but he said she'd been acting suspicious pretty much since they got off the bus. "You know that look she gets," he said.

When they noticed her missing at lunchtime, someone tattled that they saw her whispering to Jack just before she disappeared, and of course the teachers all knew how close they were anyway, so he spent the rest of the afternoon getting grilled by first one teacher and then another, good cop bad cop fashion, about what she'd said and where she'd gone.

They suspended her from school for three days for ditching the field trip, and of course her mom grounded the hell out of her. She wasn't even allowed to talk on the telephone. "Practically a prisoner on bread and water," she told me. So it was almost a week before I got to hear the whole story. She had blithely refused to let on to anyone where she had really been—not her mom, or my mom, or her teacher or the police or anyone. "I just lost track of time," was all she would say.

"But what were you doing?"

"Oh, you know, just looking around."

"Looking around where? Where did you go?"

"I don't know, just around. I don't really remember. Looking at trees and stuff. Sorry." And no matter how much they threatened, pleaded, teased or bullied her, they couldn't get any more detail out of her than that.

But to me, of course, she told the truth, as soon as we had the time in private. This is what had happened: when they were on the bus, just before they arrived at the ruins in St. Norbert, they had passed the cemetery where her grandmother once took her to see her sister's grave.

She was sure of it. She said she totally recognized the black marble gateposts at the front entrance, and the squat and twisty crabapple trees growing along the wrought iron fence. She said that the moment she saw it out the window of the bus she was a hundred percent certain it was the same graveyard, though I don't know how she could have been so sure, cemeteries all look the same to me.

So she waited until everyone was more or less engrossed in the tour, gave Jack the quick whisper, and then melted out of sight, the way she always could. She figured she'd only be gone about an hour at most—fifteen minutes to the cemetery, half an hour tops to find her sister's headstone, then fifteen minutes back, in time for lunch. If anyone noticed she had gone, she'd tell them a story about having to go to the bathroom, say she had diarrhea or something. The diarrhea bit always worked, if you got enthusiastically graphic enough they'd drop the subject and stop asking questions pretty fast.

Addy found the cemetery without difficulty, though it was a little further away than she'd judged from the bus, maybe twenty minutes walking instead of ten or fifteen. And it was exactly how she remembered it. The crabapple trees had dropped their fruit in slimy little piles along the fence; the whole place smelled like a pile of leaves that's been raked up and then left too long and starts rotting underneath, and that was how she remembered it too. It was even the same kind of day as when she and her grandmother had come there eight years before, a grey dull day, one of those flat bland sidewalk-coloured skies that nothing even seems to cast a shadow under.

There was no sign of other people around. As she headed up one row and down another, reading the inscriptions on the tombstones, she realized that it wasn't going to be as easy as she had imagined to find Maddy's grave. Addy had sort of assumed that the graves in a cemetery would be in some kind of order, maybe according to the date each person died. She had expected she would only have to skim the year of death on the headstones in order to track down her sister's grave in no time. But she quickly learned that there was no order whatsoever, people were just buried all over the place. She walked around for a while, but it was looking hopeless and it was getting late.

As she stood there thinking it over, she thought she saw, just a ways off in the distance, a headstone that looked exactly like she remembered Madeline's: same size, shape, colour, and everything. It wouldn't hurt to check. But it must have been a trick of the light, she said, because she'd thought it was only a few dozen yards away, but once she started walking towards it, it was more like a hundred yards or more before she finally tracked it down. And then, when she got right up to it, it didn't look at all the same. It was too tall, the corners were cut different, the stone was a different shade of grey. And it certainly wasn't Maddy, it was some woman named Phyllis who died back in the eighties at the age of forty-seven, and her family missed her deeply but she was gone to join her Lord.

Now this is where it got a bit confusing. Addy admitted that she had a hard time finding her way out of the cemetery again, which was unusual for her. Usually she has a pretty perfect sense of direction; but the fact is that she couldn't find the gates at all, and after wandering around for a while she eventually just said screw it and climbed over the fence.

So that's fine. But she swore, she absolutely insisted, there was no way she could have been in there longer than an hour, an hour at the absolute most, and she couldn't possibly have been gone from the field trip more than two hours. But we sat down and figured it out, and she must have been actually gone for more than seven hours. Seven! This, she insisted to me, was absolutely impossible, but impossible or not, that was the fact. That's how long she was gone. By the time she got back to the field trip, she expected to find everyone sitting down in the middle of lunch, maybe just finishing up, but the whole place was deserted. The bus had gone, the police must have been and looked around and already gone, the sun was getting low on the horizon and there was no one in sight.

So she had to walk all the way home from St. Norbert, cause she didn't have bus fare or even a quarter for a phone call. This, she told Casey, is exactly why she ought to let her have money to hang on to whenever she went out, but I don't think Casey saw it that way. And Jack, if he couldn't have convinced them to wait for her—she told him she was coming right back, didn't she?—at least he could have got them to leave her lunch bag behind for her. She hadn't eaten anything since breakfast, she was starving, and it's not like her mother ever let her have money in case of emergency so she could have bought something to eat or at least a drink. Instead she had to walk all the way home on an empty stomach, with the sun going down and her nose starting to bleed so she had to use her shirt sleeve to plug it because she didn't have any Kleenex, and meanwhile, where the hell were the cops anyway? They were supposed to be all out looking for her, but she didn't see a single cop car the entire way home. They were probably all off eating doughnuts somewhere instead of finding her and giving her a lift, and she had to walk all the way home alone, after dark, right through downtown and up some pretty sketchy streets. It would have served everybody right if she'd got raped and mugged and murdered, or passed out in a gutter from hunger pains or something.

Of course Addy intended to take the first possible opportunity to go back and explore the cemetery again. I made her promise to bring me along so I could help her look. She figured out what buses we would have to take, there wasn't a direct line so we'd have to transfer at Polo Park and it would take about an hour and a half each way. But no opportunities came along before winter did. The snow fell and the temperature dropped and we decided it was best to put it off until spring.

In the meantime, we put together a kind of supply kit, adding to it periodically. There were copies of the bus schedules and routes we'd have to use, and there was loose change for bus fare and emergencies. There were granola bars and drink boxes, strips of fruit leather and stuff like that, basically anything we could skim out of our school lunches that wouldn't go bad. There were a couple flashlights, a handful of Band-Aids and a bunch of Kleenex, a pair of cheap plastic binoculars, a Swiss army knife that I snicked out of Jack's room. We really wanted a pair of good walkie-talkies, I even asked for them for Christmas, but I got some books and a pair of new shoes instead. I thought we ought to have a compass too, but I couldn't find one and probably wouldn't have known how to use it anyway. Addy sketched out a map of the cemetery as she remembered it from her most recent visit, and then tried to recall as many details as she could from when she'd gone there with her grandma. When we were bored sometimes, we'd pull it out and look it over. She'd try to imagine where the grave might be, and what would be the most efficient way of exploring the place, the best plan of attack.

We kept the map and other things in my room, first because Addy came over to our house more often than I went to her place, and second because she never really trusted Casey not to rifle through her stuff when she was at school. And over the course of winter, any time we were bored or it was too cold out to do anything fun, we'd pull out our supply kit and map and go over the plans.

We finally went in March, one day over spring break. I don't remember where we told Mom and Casey we were supposedly going, but I remember it was still only half-light out when we left, it was cold enough to see your breath, and there were still brown and grey heaps of half-melted snow on the ground. The first bus when we got on it was packed almost to the point of suffocation, but by the time we were getting close to our destination, that second bus was practically empty. I remember thinking the bus driver was eyeing us suspiciously, but that was probably just my imagination. We ended up riding all the way out to the Ruins, where the field trip had been, without seeing the cemetery anywhere. We walked around looking for it for what felt like hours, we even stopped some people and asked them but no one knew what we were talking about, they said there had never been a cemetery anywhere around there, and finally we had to just give it up. We ate our lunches on the bus ride home, and barely spoke.

# 10

DOWN A NARROW AND COBBLESTONE STREET, ROSE AND Emmanuel were startled by a man crouched halfway up a tree. They hadn't noticed him up there, coiled and motionless amid the branches, until he screamed at them as they passed. Completely naked, his thin taut body covered with fine brown hairs and small red scabs, he continued screaming like a broken siren until they had disappeared through the next intersection.

Now that she had a destination, a direction to go, Rose walked fast—so fast that Emmanuel struggled at times to keep up with her. The pain in her legs, the blisters on her feet, the gnawing hunger and freezing cold, it hardly mattered any more. The only thing that mattered was making her way through the maze of streets as fast as possible, always turning left like Malcolm had told her, hardly even pausing at the intersections to make sure that Emmanuel made the turn at her side.

"Do you think it could be true?" Emmanuel said.

"It has to be true," said Rose, almost angrily. She thought he was talking about her sister. "It *was* Bethany, I know it was, it had to be her."

"I mean about the queen," the boy said. "Do you think she could really...you know?"

For the man had told them all about the queen, and what many people believed. He had first heard the rumours about her, he told them, many years before, how people started saying that a little girl had come here who could eat, and drink, and not throw up. She could actually sleep, and not be flooded with memories or nightmares. They said that if she got hurt, she would heal, and that she actually grew and got older, just as if she were still alive. They even said she pissed and shit and cast a shadow.

That was all people were saying back then, and no one called her "the queen" or anything like that. He didn't think about it much; he figured it was just a story, something that people had made up and told one another, just to have something to tell. One woman told him she'd heard that the girl had come here as a baby. Not even a baby, but in fact a fetus, unborn, that she had actually committed suicide when she was still in the womb, hanging herself with the umbilical cord. She had killed herself before she was even born, and that's why she was different from everybody else. That was years ago. The man had heard that maybe as long as ten years ago—ten, fifteen years ago. Of course he could only guess at how long it had been.

It was more recently, the last couple years perhaps, that he had started hearing people talk about the girl again, and calling her the queen now. They spoke about her as if she were some kind of saviour. They said that she lived in the very centre of the city—no one had ever been able to find the centre until she did—and that if you went to her there and she believed that you were worthy, she had the power to set you free, to release you from this place. What "being worthy" meant he had no idea. Release you how, or to where, of course no one could say. To nothingness, perhaps, oblivion—that would be the best imaginable thing. But then, every single person here had believed once before that they were releasing themselves to oblivion, back when they had committed suicide, "And look how well that turned out for us," the man said. "Still," he said, "you know we're all desperate for any kind of hope, you can hardly blame people for wanting to believe."

"Do you think it could be true?" Emmanuel asked her, ready to believe whatever Rose thought was right. But Rose didn't know what she wanted to believe. What if it *was* true, and Bethany had already found her, and been set free. What if Bethany was already gone, and Rose would never see her again after all? She knew that if that were true, and Bethany had been released from this terrible place, she ought to only feel happy for her sister. But every time she thought of it, it made her feel frustrated, desperate, and angry. So she tried not to think of it at all. All she wanted to think about was finding the centre of the city, and then whatever would be, would be.

"How will we even know when we get to the centre?" Emmanuel asked. "What if we walk right past it?"

"I don't know," said Rose. "I suppose we won't be able to turn left any more, but I don't know." She sounded irritated, short-tempered, and she knew it and she felt bad about it, but she couldn't help herself. Exhaustion was starting to eat at her mind; she was so tired it was getting harder and harder to think clearly. How long had she been dead, she wondered, a month, two months, maybe three at the most? It was impossible to say. How much longer would they have to walk before they found the centre? And what if, like Emmanuel said, they walked right past it? She had to fight the impulse to simply leave him behind. She could go so much faster without him and his bare feet, she thought. She could make it seem like an accident, just get ahead of him and turn a corner a little too quickly and she'd disappear. But then she hated herself for even considering it, and she knew that he was just as tired and in as much pain as she could be, and he was younger, too, and had lived a softer life before coming here. She had to be stronger than he was.

As they walked, the wind pounded at their backs, stinking of mold and rotten meat. Pools of blood and puddles of vomit were becoming more frequent along the broken ground, so that Emmanuel often had to skip or leap to avoid them. His feet were cut up in half a dozen places, with ripped blisters that oozed pus and burned with pain, but when Rose offered to let him wear her boots for a while, he stubbornly refused.

Along one street they saw a damaged face peer down at them from a second-storey window, and they stopped and called out, offering to help. It was, they thought, a woman, with muddy brown hair and a mass of blood and bone where her jaw ought to have been. They called out first in English, then again in French and

Spanish, but the face just disappeared from the window. And then, after a few moments, the woman returned and began throwing rocks and pieces of bricks down at them, and they had to turn and run, but not before Rose was struck heavily on her right and upraised forearm, leaving a vicious brown and yellow welt that surged with pain every time she moved her fingers.

Along another street they passed a brick house that had collapsed completely, a horrible muffled and unending scream coming from beneath the rubble. Their first impulse was to dig the person out, but if they did, what then? The man—it sounded like a man, judging by the screams—the man would be in no less pain. His broken bones would never heal, he'd be unable to move, and Rose and Emmanuel could hardly drag him through the streets to find the queen. There was no relief they could offer, nothing they could do to make it better, and so they hurried on, but the sound of those screams lingered in their ears a long time afterwards.

Presently they turned and emerged into a wide and open square, surrounded on three sides by a great grand limestone edifice, surrounding the square on three sides like a horseshoe. There was no way forward that they could see, only back the way they came.

The central part of the building might have been a hundred feet high or more, topped by a green dome and a flagpole, with a completely blank and ragged flag that flapped stiffly in the perpetual wind. Gargoyles ran along the gutters on either wing, doglike heads with long protruding tongues, chipped and molded and worn with age. At the top of eleven steps that ran all along the front of the building, great grey pillars rose twenty or thirty feet in the air. One had toppled down where a black fat tree grew right through the stone, and now lay smashed into heavy chunks along the stairs. On either side of the steps perched a life-sized statue of a lion, the one on their right lying down in magisterial repose and the one on their left standing, leaning backwards as though coiled and ready to spring.

The white and yellow walls of the building were eaten away in places by a black and encroaching mold. Everywhere else they were covered, up to eight or nine feet high, in drawings, painted in blood: a great chaotic panoply of animals and birds, lizards, insects, fish and fanciful monsters, and of men and women eating and drinking, feasting at tables laid with roast chicken and bowls of soup, bread, cheese, and cake, glasses of wine and bottles of beer, or else engaged in sex, or sometimes both at once.

To their left, a young man and a young woman sat on the steps, huddled close together by the feet of the lion, one raincoat spread over both their shoulders; the woman had her face nestled against the man's shoulder, and the man kissed the woman gently on the top of her head. On the gallery to their right, beneath the tree and beside the standing lion, three men sat on chunks of the broken pillar, talking quietly. One low branch of the tree had been snapped, and it pulsed out blood that ran down the trunk and flowed in a rivulet down the steps to pool in the square.

There was an older woman who sat on the gallery in the wide deep central doorway, a little apart from the others, perched on a chunk of pillar that must have been moved across for the purpose. Her back was against the tall oak doors, and she beckoned for Rose and Emmanuel to approach with a languid, imperial gesture.

She was a large woman, with a great straight nose like a doorstop and a neck so long it made Rose think of a camel. Her grey and copper hair was piled and pinned on the top of her head like a fantastic tower, the better perhaps to show off her dangling long diamond earrings. She wore a ruffled and elaborate purple gown, surprisingly well preserved, and a chunky diamond and emerald necklace nestled in her plump, freckled cleavage; on every one of her fingers, even her thumbs, she wore two or more gold rings, encrusted with jewels of every kind and colour. She had one large ulcer on her swollen lower lip, and three or four raw and pustular open sores, about the size of a nickel, on the palms of her hands; when she spoke, they caught a glimpse of another just like them, along the top of her tongue.

"Why," she said to them as they neared, "You're nothing but children, both of you." Her voice was low, warm and rolling.

"Are you the queen?" Emmanuel asked impulsively, a hint of awe in his voice, but the woman laughed.

"No, my child, I'm not the queen. I'm not even *a* queen, not even when I was alive." She turned her gaze now to Rose, and said, "You are a beautiful child, though." She caressed the sore on her lip with the tip of her tongue as she looked Rose over thoughtfully. Her eyes were grey and her eyelids heavy and smeared with red, as if she had been using someone or something's blood for makeup. "And what is your name, child?"

"Rose," she said. "And this is my friend, Emmanuel." She slipped her left hand over his.

"Rose?" said the woman disapprovingly. "You look nothing like a rose, child. A beautiful flower, yes, but not a rose, no. No, no thorns on you. We shall call you Lily, like a lovely water lily, a nymph. And you must stay with us, here where it is safe. You can throw away those ugly boots, you won't need them any more."

As she spoke, Rose noticed that the men had stood up from their seats beneath the tree and were quietly approaching; not interrupting, or coming too close, but discreetly listening and looking over the newcomers. And she noticed that none of them were bleeding, nor showed any gross signs of how they'd died.

"Please, ma'am," she began to say, trying to choose her words carefully so as not to inadvertently cause offense, but the woman interrupted her.

"My name here is Sophonisba," she said grandly. "Sophonisba Pieralvise. But you may call me Sophia. You shall like it here, Lily, we have only beautiful things around us, and we make it peaceful here, as peaceful as we may." Leaning forward, she reached out her hand and caressed the bruise on Rose's forearm tenderly, then closed her fingers gently but firmly over Rose's wrist. Rose was glad that, when she was alive, she'd had to learn how not to show fear or disgust on her face or in her body, only blankness, for it was a skill she needed now.

"You won't get any more ugly bruises here," the woman continued. "I shan't let you get damaged any further, my child." And then turning to the men, she said, "Come, bring Lily a seat, and help her remove her boots. You must tell me your story, child," Sophia went on, turning back to Rose, her hand squeezing the girl's wrist a little more firmly now, so that it sent a throb of pain up her forearm, and Rose could feel the cold metal of the woman's rings and the sticky sores on her palms pressing against her flesh.

"Your skin is like ice, child," Sophia said tenderly, rubbing the skin of Rose's wrist with her thumb. "How can you be so cold?" She paid no more attention to Emmanuel whatsoever, as though she'd decided to pretend he didn't exist, and the men—two of whom were rolling a section of the broken pillar along the gallery towards them, while the third had moved around to stand behind Rose and Emmanuel now, a few feet back—the men seemed to pay little or no attention to him either. Rose gave his hand a reassuring squeeze and he returned the pressure, making her palm sting where it was cut, and the blood oozed out between their fingers.

"I am composing a poem, you know, Lily. In terza rima, to challenge myself. Memory here is a marvelous thing, my poem is more than forty-seven thousand verses and I remember every one, word for perfect word. I shall sing it to you presently, and you shall weep, Lily, for it is very sad and beautiful. And then I shall add your story to it. I'm sure it must be a sad and lovely story, that such a beautiful child as you should choose to die. Tell me, Lily," she said, drawing Rose a little closer and tonguing the sore on her lip again, "Was it a man? A broken promise, a shattered reputation?"

The men had finished bringing the section of pillar around now, setting it in the doorway right next to Sophia. The man who was standing behind them stepped forward and placed his hands on Emmanuel's shoulders, pulling him back and away as the other two men took Rose and gently but forcibly seated her. One of the men then kneeled down and began the hard work of undoing the knots in her blood-soaked bootlaces. Nor all this time did Sophia once let go of her wrist or relax her grip.

"Please," said Rose again, "I should love to stay with you, and hear your poem, but I need to find my sister. That's why I came here," she hurried on before the woman could interrupt her again. "*That's* why I chose to die, so I could see my sister again."

The man yanked her right boot from her foot, and handed it the other, who walked a little ways up the gallery, and tossed it high in the air and through an open window.

Sophia had shifted around in her seat so that she was facing Rose. Still holding her by the wrist, she placed her other hand over Rose's and began gently massaging her palm. "Yes," she said, almost purring, her heavy lids low over her eyes. "Tell me about your sister, Lily."

So Rose did, laying emphasis on how beautiful Bethany was, and how everyone always fell in love with her as soon as they met her, and told in great detail how she herself had discovered her sister's body in the closet. Sophia listened intently, not interrupting but often forming silent words with her lips, as though repeating certain phrases that Rose spoke, perhaps amending their meter or thinking of possible rhymes. And meanwhile Rose's other boot had gone the same way as the first, tossed through the high open window and irretrievable, and the man kneeling before her began tenderly wiping her feet with a rag.

Everyone was listening to Rose's story closely, including the young man and young woman who had been sitting together beneath the raincoat, but who had now drawn closer to join the rest. One of the men still stood behind Emmanuel, his hands resting on the boy's shoulders, though not quite holding him. Emmanuel himself looked wretched, small, useless and confused. Rose tried to give him a reassuring glance, but in truth she didn't feel very assured herself. All she could do was continue her story. She told them about her own death, in Beaconsfield Park beneath the snow, and how she had searched for Bethany ever since she had been here, and only just recently had found someone who had seen her, travelling with a group of pilgrims, trying to find the queen.

When she mentioned the queen, she thought she saw the men and the young woman all exchange glances—some frowning, or looking uncomfortable, some smiling slightly as though secretly amused. But the expression on Sophia's face did not change, nor her eyes shift for even a moment off Rose's face, but she said solemnly, "You know that the queen is a lie, child, a fairy tale that fools believe in. There is no queen, and no one will come to 'save' us."

"I don't care about the queen," said Rose firmly, but she found that there were tears forming in her eyes despite herself, and she had to sniff twice. "I don't care whether the queen is real or not, I only want to find my sister. Perhaps," she said, "when we find her,"—and she made a point of saying "we," glancing over at Emmanuel when she said it—"Perhaps when we find her, we can bring her back here with us, and all stay here together."

Now Sophia smiled sadly, and squeezed Rose's hand hard enough that it hurt a little, and said gently, "And how would you find us again, child?"

"We could try," Rose said firmly. "We'd have forever, wouldn't we? Sooner or later we'd find our way back, and you would still be here, wouldn't you?"

"It would make a great story for your poem," said Emmanuel loudly and suddenly, speaking for the very first time, and Sophia looked over at him with as much surprise as if a dog or a cat had suddenly spoken to her. "How she found Bethany, and they were reunited, and returned here and stuff," he went on, a little less boldly now that they were all looking at him, and stammering slightly.

"Yes," Sophia said, with a certain formal coldness to her voice. "But you see, I could add that to my poem anyway, whether it actually happens or not." And then she gave the slightest of bows in the boy's direction, and returned her attention to Rose. "Tell me now, Lily, how you got that ugly bruise on your poor arm."

Rose told her about the woman in the window, and Sophia said, "You see, child? That is nothing compared to what could happen if I let you continue. The closer you get to the centre, the more people like that you will encounter. Savages, child, savages crazed with pain, or crazy to begin with, who would think of nothing but making you as ugly as they are—people who would rain down on you with rocks or batter you with sticks and bricks, slash you with knives and razors, bite you or claw you like an animal, try to eat your sweet flesh even—you simply can't imagine, Lily, a pure sweet innocent child like you, the horrors you would encounter. If your sister really has gone that way... and it pains me, child, to have to say this, but if your sister really has gone to the centre, she has probably already been maimed and mutilated beyond help or recognition."

"Stop that," said the young woman, abruptly, angrily, stepping forward. "How can you be so mean?" And Rose and Emmanuel looked at her for the first time, really. She was quite tall, and terribly pale, thin and weak looking. Her hair was so blonde it might have looked almost white in direct sunlight, straight and fine and cut quite short; her eyes were a wide and watery sort of blue, her face round as a doll's, her mouth small and puckered. She looked like she might have been twenty-five when she died, and her voice was startlingly high-pitched, almost squeaky. She was so angry that she trembled.

Sophia smiled at her condescendingly, and said to Rose, "This is Alexandria. She has a good heart, as you can see, but I'm afraid she isn't terribly bright."

"I am not," said the young woman. "My name is Alison, you stupid old bitch." The man she had been sitting with, the man who had kissed her, opened his mouth to say something, and then apparently thought better of it, and stepped back a little, looking away as if hoping not to be noticed.

"Alexandria," the old woman said firmly, "I know that it sounds cruel, but I am only telling Lily these truths for her own protection."

"Bullshit," said Alison firmly. "Don't you listen to her," she squeaked to Rose. "She's a disgusting old pig, and her poem is horrible and boring."

Sophia's cheeks flamed with rage. She dropped Rose's hand and began laboriously trying to get to her feet. One of the men—the one who had been standing behind Emmanuel—stepped towards Alison, hand out-stretched, and when Alison saw him approaching, she flew suddenly forward, faster than anyone could catch her, her long and jagged fingernails outstretched, scratching the old woman across the face and knocking her over backwards. They tumbled together in a heap against the doorway and rolled and clawed and bit at one another, both shrieking hideously. The men rushed in to try and separate them, and Rose and Emmanuel ran down the stairs and away from the square as fast as their bare feet would carry them, Rose grabbing on to Emmanuel's hand and holding tight as they turned the corner.

# 11

IN OCTOBER JACK GOT SUSPENDED FROM SCHOOL FOR TWO days, this time for bringing a stray dog into the building. He swore up and down that he was innocent, he didn't know how the dog got in, but they suspended him anyway.

The dog was big and yellow and obviously starving, Jack said you could see the poor thing's ribs sticking out through its fur. It pissed in the hallway, went nuts in the lunchroom, and bit the physics teacher on the hand before they managed to corral it in the boys' washroom and call Animal Control. Only by the time Animal Control got there the dog had somehow disappeared, leaving behind a big fat crap on the middle of the floor, and they blamed Jack for that too, for helping the dog escape though he said he doesn't know how he could have, with the caretaker and the vice-principal guarding the washroom door the entire time, but he admitted he was glad it got away. The physics teacher had to get five stitches on his hand and a whack of shots.

Then it was my turn, and one day at the end of October, I remember it was a Thursday, when I got to school in the morning they told me to go straight to the vice-principal's office.

I was later than usual that morning, too. This was just a day or two after the first snow, and I wasn't really dressed for it, so after I'd walked with Jack and Conrad to the high school like always, when the bell rang for classes to begin I slipped inside and hid in the washroom to warm up. I must have lingered in there longer than I realized—there were a couple older girls having a pretty interesting conversation I kinda wanted to hear the end of. Anyway, I was half an hour late by the time I arrived at my school, and when I tried to slip into my first class the teacher hardly even glanced up to see who was opening the door, he just said, "Natalie, Mr. Benson is waiting for you in his office."

When I got to his office, the secretary told me to go straight in with that kind of sorry half-smile she'd give you when she knew you were in trouble, and there was my mom, sitting in a chair they'd pulled up beside his desk, looking totally homicidal. It was an ambush.

I found out later they'd arranged it over the phone two days before, and Mom didn't say anything to me, she hadn't let on at all. I mean, I guess in retrospect she had been acting weird around me those last couple days, getting angry at me for no apparent reason, and then the night before Davey had tried to corner me and have a big serious talk, asking me if I had anything on my mind I wanted to share with him, any problems at school or boys or stuff like that. But with Mom all pregnant and stressed and hormonal and stuff, she and Davey used to act weird like that all the time, for no reason at all. How was I supposed to guess that this time there was something behind it, and they'd had a call about me from Mr. Benson?

Anyway, Mom didn't say anything the whole time we were in that office, she just sat there, pouting like crazy and kind of glaring at me, while Mr. Benson lectured me about cutting classes, and coming late and leaving early, and showing respect, and slippery slopes, and permanent records. Mom looked so angry the whole time I thought she might vomit. The only time she spoke was to tell me to stop chewing my nails.

I think Mr. Benson was a little surprised or, I don't know, disconcerted maybe that Mom was so totally silent. He kept pausing and looking over at her, in case she wanted to add something, but she never did. By now the bell had rung for my second class already, so I was going to be late for that one, too.

When he kind of ran out of things to repeat, there was a long awkward silence, and he finally said, "Ms. Wellesley? What do you think?"

Mom said, in a really cold voice and still staring at me, glaring at me, she said, "I think Natalie and I are going to have a long, long talk this evening. And I don't think you're going to have any more problems with her." Then she thanked him politely and asked him where the bathroom was. He popped to his feet like a jack-in-the-box and offered his hand to show her the way. I think being around a really pregnant woman made him pretty nervous.

Mom and I had a huge fight that night. She went on about how she was going to have enough to worry about with a new baby coming to take care of, and the last thing she needed was to have to worry about me and Jack acting like idiot teenagers, and how I'd better start growing up and taking responsibility for myself.

I was pretty angry, too. I felt like it just wasn't that big a deal, it's not like I was failing any of my classes or anything, my grades were okay, so who cares? All my friends were at high school already, I just wanted to hang out with them a little bit. Why did it have to be such a huge issue?

And then Mom said, "Those are *Jack's* friends. Don't you have any of your own?" Which I thought was hurtful and not even true, and I really was angry then, and I started yelling at her, telling her she didn't understand anything and she was just taking it out on me because she was all knocked up and miserable, and poor Davey sitting there in the middle of it, trying to calm us both down and have a reasonable discussion, and he didn't even have a beer.

And Mom was yelling too, saying things like, "Why do you always want to be older? Why are you in such a hurry to grow up?" which I thought was just completely stupid and it proved she didn't understand anything, and it also completely contradicted what she'd just told me ten minutes ago about how I'd better start growing up, and I told her that, and she just went on, saying, "Why don't you have any friends your own age? What about that girl, Rose? You used to hang out with her all the time last year."

Davey had to tell her that Rose was Jack's age, not mine, and in high school too, and Mom looked embarrassed for half a second, and then said, "See what I mean? That's exactly my point." Like she'd made the mistake on purpose.

The upshot of it all was that I wouldn't be allowed to walk to school in the mornings any more. Davey would drive me right to the front doors every day and watch me go in. "And he'll walk you to your first class and sit you the hell down at your desk and open your book for you if he has to," Mom added, and if they heard from Mr. Benson that I was missing any more classes or cutting out early again, I'd be grounded for the rest of the school year, which was totally ridiculous. She even threatened to tell Addy she wasn't allowed to come for Christmas if I didn't straighten up. As it was, I was grounded for the weekend, which made me extra furious because it meant I couldn't go to the big Gate Night party at Conrad's house on Saturday, and they knew it. They did it that way on purpose, and I went to my room and slammed my door and didn't say a single word to either of them until Tuesday or something. I wasn't allowed to use the phone either, so I couldn't even call Addy and bitch about it.

It was going to be the best party ever, too, because Conrad's parents and Nana weren't going to be there, and his older brothers were going to be in charge. He had three older brothers, and they were all totally different from him, they all took after their dad—big and hairy and smelly like a bunch of house baboons—while Conrad took after his mom. Except that Boris, his dad, was completely sweet and everybody loved him. He was like a big, dumb, stinky dog who one minute he's barking at you and scaring the crap out of you, and the next minute he's jumping up and putting his paws on your shoulder and licking your face. He used to swear a blue streak, which sounded pretty funny cause he had that weird Afrikaner accent that would come out when he's drunk, and he was always telling us bizarre and pretty inappropriate stories about things he saw on his job as a garbage man, or these racist, terrible, funny stories from back when he lived in South Africa as a kid—not that he was racist himself. He and Davey were great buddies, they loved having a pile of beer together. Conrad's oldest brother Theo was the most like Boris that way. We liked *him*, but he'd taken off to Vancouver as soon as he turned eighteen, so that left Peter and Ben, who were both just totally disgusting, burping, farting, slobbering animals, and *they* were going to be in charge of the party. They'd probably invite a bunch of their own friends over and score booze and everything, and Jack and I had gotten permission to spend the whole night and come home in the morning, because I don't think Mom realized that Conrad's parents weren't going to be there. Davey might have known from Boris but if he did he didn't say anything. And now I couldn't go at all.

I fantasized about sneaking out, maybe through my bedroom window, and going after all, but I don't think I really seriously considered it. Addy could do that kind of thing easy as breathing and even get away with it, but I'd probably have gotten caught before I got past our back yard. I didn't really think Mom would follow through on her threat to not let Addy come for Christmas, but I didn't want to take the chance; and even if I had gotten away with it, I probably wouldn't have enjoyed myself, I'd have been too nervous and angry and guilty-feeling the whole time there. Mom and Davey rented a couple horror movies and made popcorn and invited me to watch with them, but I still wasn't speaking to them. All I wanted to do was shut myself in my room and lie on my bed feeling sorry for myself and angry at everyone, and that's exactly what I did.

I fell asleep so early that I woke up stupid early, like five-thirty or something, with the wind hucking ice at my bedroom window, and I couldn't get back to sleep. So I was awake and sitting in the kitchen eating cereal when Jack came home, hoping to sneak in and not see anyone. He smelled a bit like stale booze and skunkweed, but I don't think he was drunk or high. But his lower lip had opened again in the same place he had to get stitches the year before, and there was blood all down his chin and the front of his jacket.

I said, "Holy shit, what happened to you? Did you get in a fight or something?" And he said, "Nothing, it's nothing. Don't tell Mom," kind of irritably, but I think he was feeling sorry for me, getting grounded and missing out, so he was making an effort to be nice.

And then I said, "Holy shit, was *Bridget* at the party?" and he got pissed off at that, and he said, "No, Bridget wasn't at the party. It's nothing, it just opened up because of the cold, okay?" And he went upstairs, taking his coat with him, and locked himself in his room and stayed there all day, until dinner. Which made me wonder if maybe Bridget really *had* been at the party.

Bridget was this girl he'd been going with the year before. She was his first, and so far his only, girlfriend. They had met over the Christmas holidays, I don't remember where, at the movies or hanging out at the mall or something, and they were pretty serious for a couple months. To tell you the truth, I didn't like her all that much—or it wasn't that I didn't *like* her, she was certainly nice enough, I just couldn't understand what Jack saw in her for a girlfriend. Every girl I knew had a crush on my brother, he could have dated basically anyone he wanted, what was so special about Bridget? She really wasn't very bright, she didn't read books or anything, and I didn't even think she was all that pretty, I kind of thought she looked like a chipmunk, but Jack was seriously into her.

I know Mom felt the same way about her that I did. Maybe if we'd spent more time with her we would have learned to like her better, or started to see what Jack saw in her, but she didn't come to our house very often. Her aunt and uncle liked Jack, but they thought we lived in a sketchy neighbourhood, so he usually went to their house to hang out.

Davey always said that Mom and I were both being unfair and unkind. He said that Bridget didn't look anything like a chipmunk, she was obviously adorable, and that there were worse things in the world than not being bright and not reading lots of books. And anyway, we *did* live in a sketchy neighbourhood, her aunt and uncle were perfectly correct, so you couldn't hold that against them, and as long as Jack liked her and he was happy then that was the only thing that mattered.

Bridget lived with her aunt and uncle because when she was nine, she had been taken into foster care; her father wasn't in the picture and I guess her mother had problems. So the social workers took her away and at first they put her into a motel and kept her there until they could find a home for her.

On the third day in the motel a man came to visit her, they said he was her Uncle Greg, her father's youngest brother, and maybe he was. They told her she'd met him before but she would have been just a baby, way too young to remember. He had a short visit and he seemed nice enough, and then he went away.

All this time, you know, Bridget was being very quiet, polite, did whatever people asked her to do, didn't let anyone see her cry, just went into a shell cause that seemed safest. She didn't exactly want to go back to her mother, but she didn't want to go live in some stranger's house either.

A couple days later her Uncle Greg came back, for a longer visit this time, and then again the next day. She had liked him, she told Jack, he reminded her of her father but without the frightening bits, and he was funny and laid-back, and he didn't talk down to her or say idiotic things about her feelings. She realized that there was a good chance they'd be sending her to live with him, and she had decided she liked that idea, or that at least it would be better than any of the other alternatives she could imagine.

Anyway, towards the end of this third visit the social worker left them alone for a few minutes, five or ten minutes, and Uncle Greg explained that he wanted to take her home to live with him, maybe in a week or two if they could get through all the red tape, but he needed her help.

He was trying to negotiate a good price for fostering her, but they kept low-balling him because she was too well behaved, everybody figured she'd be easy to take care of. So he needed her to start acting out. Nothing too obvious, just start misbehaving here and there, make herself difficult to deal with. She could steal some money from one of the social workers, he suggested, or run away for a few hours, or cut herself a bit or something. It was, he pointed out, in her own best interest. The more money he got paid for her, the more money he could spend on her. Then the worker came back in the room and Uncle Greg got up and said goodbye, gave her a wink, and promised to bring his wife with him to visit the next day so she could meet her.

Bridget decided to do what her uncle had asked her to, because she didn't want him to change his mind about taking her in, and then who the hell knew where she might end up?

It was hard at first, trying to basically overcome a lifelong habit of being nice and never upsetting anyone, she had to really dig down deep and force herself. The first thing she did was call the social worker a bitch, totally out of the blue, and then she burst into tears because it sounded so ridiculous and unconvincing coming out of her mouth, she said. The next day she refused to eat any food, and the third time they tried to give her something to eat she threw it across the room and called the woman a bitch again.

She told Jack that the more she forced herself to misbehave the easier it got, partly because she realized that nothing really bad was going to happen to her no matter what she did, no one was going to punish her or do anything except talk boring bullshit to her and they were doing that all the time anyway. And then after a few days of it she realized it wasn't just getting easier, she was actually starting to enjoy it. On the sixth day of being bad she bit the social worker on the arm.

She had no idea why, she said, it wasn't something she had thought about and then worked up the courage for it like the rest of the stuff she'd been doing. In fact she had sort of decided that she needed to tone it down a bit, cause maybe if she acted out *too* much they might figure Uncle Greg wouldn't be able to handle her at all, and they'd put her in an institution or something—she'd seen her aunt and uncle that morning, and they'd hinted as much, told her she was doing great and they were proud of her, but don't overdo it, now.

So for the rest of the day Bridget had made an effort to be nice again; and then, at bedtime, when the social worker tucked the blanket over her and sat on the side of the bed and started saying kind, caring things to her, Bridget told Jack that something just came over her, and she sat suddenly up and bit the woman on the forearm and wouldn't let go until she got some blood in her mouth. She admitted to Jack that it was the best thing she ever tasted in her life, salty and rusty and warm and delicious. She never bit anyone again—well, not until Jack, anyway, but she would lie in bed sometimes at night, hugging the memory of the flavour of it in her mind as she drifted off sweetly to sleep.

Anyway, one evening Jack was at her house and they were making out on the couch in the basement and she bit his lip. Not just a little nip like normal, this time she practically tore half his lower lip off, and the blood was pouring down his chin and neck and she was, like, lapping at it until he pushed her away, because it hurt like a son-of-a-bitch. Then she was afraid to let her aunt and uncle see what had happened, so he had to sneak out of the house with a hand towel over his face while she cleaned up.

He took the bus home, bleeding all over the place, and it was so cold—this was the end of February—it was so cold the blood froze the towel to his face. Of course he didn't want to tell us what had happened even though Davey had to take him to the hospital so they could clean it up and stitch his lip back on, and Mom was freaking out completely. He probably would have never told us anything, but Davey said the doctor could tell it was a human bite just by looking at it, and we all knew where he'd been, so the truth had to come out after that.

They broke up, but the funny thing was that *she* broke up with *him*. Of course Mom forbade Jack to ever see her again, but that wouldn't have stopped him, he was still really into her. It was Bridget who did the breaking; in fact she didn't even really break up with him, she just stopped answering his calls and ignored his messages and she wouldn't talk to him or anything. He took the bus out to her place one day after school when he told Mom he was going over to Conrad's, and her uncle came to the door and threatened to call the police if he ever showed up there again.

Jack never, ever did tell me what happened at that Gate Night party. I had to get the story from Conrad a few days later. And it turned out it wasn't Bridget after all. Bridget hadn't been at the party, like I suspected, no one we knew had heard from her since she and Jack broke up. But Rose was at the party, looking so much like her big sister now it was kind of uncanny, Conrad said, and even acting like her a little, or maybe not so much acting like her as just giving off that same kind of vibe that Bethany used to.

It was getting around the end of the night and the party was winding down. Conrad's brothers were starting to give people rides home and stuff, and Rose and Jack sort of disappeared together for a little bit. Conrad didn't really think about it, he told me, cause he was too busy trying to get shit cleaned up in case his parents came home, but the two of them were probably gone for about half an hour before they came running out of one of the bedrooms, and their mouths were both all slobbered with blood. I asked him, but he wasn't sure if Rose ran out first and Jack followed her, or if it was the other way around.

I thought it would be pretty cool if Jack and Rose started seeing each other, like boyfriend-girlfriend sort of thing, but as far as I could find out nothing happened after, it was just a one-time thing. Of course Jack wouldn't talk about it, he never talked to me about anything. And I wasn't allowed to hang out at the high school any more, or I might have tried to talk to Rose herself, ask *her* what had happened at the party. I wish I'd done it anyway, went and tracked her down and really talked to her, whether I got in trouble for it or not.

# 12

ROSE HAD TO WALK MORE SLOWLY NOW, HER FEET STINGING with each step, watching the ground carefully for sharp rocks and broken glass, thistles and splinters of wood, keeping close by Emmanuel's side. The dilapidated houses and buildings around them, in some streets made of brick or great slabs of stone, in others rickety slats of rotten wood, were often broken right in—not just the windows busted, but the walls and doors staved in as well, leaving great gaping holes as though it were a war zone, or the aftermath of a hurricane.

Often they saw glimpses of people hiding inside the buildings, or sifting through the rubble. Rose herself stopped at the site of a wooden house that was half collapsed, and hunted around until she found the perfect length of wood, wrenching it from a busted window frame, two feet long, an inch thick either way, and one fat rusted nail protruding from the splintered end.

They saw more graffiti, too, mostly written in blood but sometimes etched laboriously into the wood. *Come to the Queen*, it would say, or *the Green Eyed Queen Will Set You Free*. Across one splintered door someone had written, *Fuck the Queen*. Often they saw messages written in languages that neither of them could read, letters they couldn't even recognize. They saw one in Chinese or Japanese carved into the trunk of a tree, so that blood constantly filled and overflowed the words, spilling down the bark and across the ground; something too in Cyrillic, carved in a wall beneath a window, that a lean and angry man in rags was impotently trying to deface with a snapped and rusty steak knife.

The further they walked the more people they saw, many of them holding crude weapons like Rose. They had to take great care at every intersection so as not to startle anyone, or bump into them from behind, and as the streets grew more narrow and crowded, they would often have to press themselves against the walls to let others pass.

Rose scanned the faces of everyone they saw, looking for her sister among them, but she didn't speak to anyone, and avoided making eye contact. Whenever someone tried to speak to them, in any language, Rose would grab Emmanuel's arm and hurry forward, not answering, gripping the stick tightly in her other hand and perhaps lifting it a little, warningly. So, too, did most people hurry away at their approach. Few people tried to speak, and a shoddy and universal fear clouded every face: haggard, anxious and miserable, battered, strained, pained and paranoid.

Almost every road that they turned down now was a dirt road so soaked with centuries of blood and vomit that it had been churned into a thick paste. Great heavy clumps of the bloody mud clung to their feet, making it hard to walk, and a hot stink rose from the ground.

The wind pounded in their ears with such a roar and cacophony of distorted cries and distant screams that they had to almost yell to speak to one another. The trees were tall and thick, sometimes growing close enough together to almost block the road, and then they had to clamber over the gnarled roots. And there was hardly a tree they passed that didn't have one or more branches torn from it or words carved into it, pulsing out that warm black blood and giving off a pained and high-pitched shriek and a stink like sour milk.

Occasionally now they would come to an intersection that only allowed them to go forward or turn right, or sometimes only turn right. Always at the end of the next street they would find a left turn open to them, but even so, Rose felt hopeful. "We must be getting close," she said to Emmanuel, "We must be getting near the centre."

The next time they came to a corner that only turned to the right, just a few streets later, they tried turning around and walking back down the street in the other direction. They'd entered the street off a four-way crossing, but after a few hundred feet going back the way they came, they found themselves at another right-hand only turn.

"We *have* to be getting close," Rose said again. The houses on this street were the barest hovels, practically huts, hardly taller than they were, with thatched roofs half-tumbled in and windows that had never had glass, just small crude squares cut in the walls. They tried peering in through the windows, and saw nothing but bare and empty wooden rooms with dirt floors and no other exits.

"What if we go between them?" Emmanuel suggested. "Turn left anyway, even if there isn't a street to turn left down, you know?" There was a gap of perhaps two feet between each house, crowded with tall thick tangled weeds, burdocks and nettles as high as their necks. Emmanuel went first, for less of his skin was exposed, and Rose followed close behind, holding on to the tail of his jacket. They stepped slowly and carefully, but couldn't help getting dozens of painful scratches and barbs in their legs and feet.

They emerged from the tangle of weeds onto a white and winding narrow street where, for the first time in a long time, no other people were to be seen. The short, close houses seemed to be made of crumbling sand, and the wind swirled the white sand into their stinging eyes and noses, and none of the houses had doors, only open doorways and no sign of people inside any of them. The trees were thin and leafless and barkless and smooth and hard as iron, every branch ending in a treacherous point. And at the end of that street, they didn't come to an intersection at all; they came to a great wall of smooth white rock, unmarked and a set of stairs cut into the stone, winding up.

"Could this be it?" Emmanuel said. "Could this be the middle?"

"I don't know," said Rose. Her brain told her not to get her hopes up, it probably wouldn't be so simple, so straightforward, but she couldn't help feeling a little hopeful despite herself. "I don't know," she said again. "I guess we're going to find out."

The stairs were steep, and far too narrow for them to walk side by side, so Rose went first, climbing slowly, using her weapon as a walking stick, and Emmanuel kept close behind her. The stairs seemed to go on forever, turning sharply to the left every eleventh step. But after perhaps half a dozen of these turns, they realized they were somehow going down now instead of up, though neither could say when the change in direction had come, and they were still turning left at every eleventh step. The top of the wall always seemed to be about fifteen or twenty feet above them, no matter how high or how low they had climbed. They could see the dull grey sky above them, but never a sight of buildings, people or trees, and there was no wind. The only blood, the drips and footprints Rose and Emmanuel left behind them.

A few more turns and the steps grew less steep, and wide enough that Emmanuel could now walk by Rose's side. Then they could see the backs of wooden houses at the tops of the walls, and red and black-red blood trickled down those walls in little rivulets, down the walls and over the steps, making them slick and treacherous. Then the stairs and the walls became soft and rotting wood instead of stone, though again neither of them could say exactly when it had changed, and they emerged at last, onto a wooden platform, like a wharf, where two dozen or more people stood or sat crowded unhappily together, crumpled and sullen.

The wharf was perhaps a hundred square feet, at most. It extended out over a river or canal of dark red blood, flowing to their left, choppy with waves and reeking with heat and putrescence. It stank like rust and rancid bacon. Bits of debris were carried along by the current, shingles and broken boards that spun swiftly by, sometimes leaping up in the waves made by the swirling wind, dancing in the foamy red spray as if they were alive. The canal was lined on either side by serried and ramshackle wooden buildings that leaned precariously over the depths, as far as the eye could see in either direction: skinny, shabby, crowded and decrepit, in many places jutting right out over the edge and held barely in place by a buttress of two-by-fours. Here and there along the wall of the canal, between the houses, you could see the blood streaming down to swell the stream.

There was no way to walk along the edge of the canal, and the only way forward was a narrow bridge of ropes and planks that swayed unsteadily, extending off one end of the wharf and stretching the forty or fifty feet across the river of blood to another landing, also crowded with people. A lone man stood at the middle of the bridge, holding a sawed-off shotgun. His head was a pulpy mess, like a ball of chopped raw meat; it gaped in two halves, hanging by sinews and skin from the stalk of his neck. His body was drenched in blood that pulsed like a fountain from his neck and poured down to the river below; and he swayed drunkenly as he stood. But he could still see, for he would lift half his head with one hand and point his one remaining eye in whatever direction he wanted to look, and his moist soft brains clung tenaciously to the inside of his fragmented skull.

"Well, here's a likely pair of heroes," said a young man standing close by as Rose and Emmanuel emerged onto the wharf, the planks beneath their feet creaking ominously. Sprightly and restless, he had his hands in his pockets and rope marks around his neck. His eyes were small and black and errant, the left one looking steadily in and down towards his nose, the right one darting briskly in every direction. "Aaron," he said, "do you suppose this pair might have a gun between them?"

"I don't," said a man in blue and grey striped silk pajamas, perched on a bollard. He was young, too, with a thin and patchy fringe of beard that looked like tufts of pubic hair glued on a lump of unbaked bread dough. His right hand was all charred and black, with a raw festering hole in the centre of his palm.

"A rifle, maybe, under that jacket?"

"Probably not."

"It's an awfully big jacket for the boy, Aaron."

"It is, Michael."

"Perhaps one of those delicate little nickel-plated ladies' pistols, do you think, tucked away in the young lady's dress?'

"I doubt she could hide much in that dress, Michael."

"You'd be surprised what a lady in a little dress could hide and you wouldn't know it, though. They have their ways, Aaron. Remind me later and I'll tell you a story about a young woman, a wee slip of a skirt, and a big fat bible."

"Sure, you told me that one already, two and a half times now."

"Well then, maybe they'd have a bow and arrow between them, do you imagine? We could make do with a bow and arrow."

"Did you ever meet a man yet who killed himself with a bow and arrow?" said Aaron, shifting uncomfortably on the bollard. "I don't think you could even do it if you tried. It'd be a good trick to kill yourself with a bow and arrow. I'd have paid a good deal of green money to see a man do that on the stage."

"I'll tell you the secret," said Michael. "Long legs, flexible toes, plenty of practice."

"It'd be a tricky business to be practising. By the time you get the hang of it, it's too late to book the theatre and print the tickets."

"You could wear a face mask, and put a wee rubber thing on the end of the arrows."

"I suppose you could, that."

"So you admit, Aaron, the young folks just might have a bow and arrow on them, then?"

"Why don't you ask them, Michael? They're more likely to know than I am."

So turning at last to Rose and Emmanuel, he said, "Pardon me, young lady, young gentleman, but you wouldn't happen to have a gun or bow of any sort about you, would you?"

"With ammunition," added Aaron.

"Ah, my friend makes a good point. With ammunition. Not so useful without it, not in this particular situation."

Rose shook her head no.

"Sure, I expected that, I'm afraid. Still, you're very welcome, of course. Pull yourselves up a piece of jetty and make yourselves comfortable, you'll probably be here a while."

"What's going on?" Emmanuel asked.

"The young gentleman would like to know what's going on," he said to Aaron

"I'm sure he would," said Aaron. "It's a natural question."

"Perfectly natural," Michael said agreeably.

"Why don't you tell him, then?"

"What's going on," said Michael to Emmanuel, "is that happy fellow down there on the bridge is going on, with his brains spilling out and a bit of shotgun in his hand. He seems to be under the impression that it's his personal bridge, that bridge, and no one else ought to be thinking of using it. Seems rather inclined to shoot anyone who might try it, and since we haven't met anyone yet who seems interested in maybe ending up looking like he does, we're all fairly stuck."

"What does he want?" Emmanuel asked.

"Ah, that we don't know. That's what we like to call 'a mystery.' Doesn't seem to want to talk about it, this fellow. Not a chatty fellow at all. Very close, in fact. Of course to be fair, I'm not so sure he's got any tongue left in that mess of a head."

"It's important to be fair," said Aaron.

"That's right, young man," Michael said to Emmanuel. "You should always be fair. Let that be a lesson to you. Still, sooner or later someone's bound to come along with a gun—"

"With ammunition."

"—with, as my friend here likes to point out, ammunition, and then maybe we can persuade the poor fellow to step aside and let people get across. Hopefully, before so many folks are all crammed on this little jetty it just collapses underneath us. Though of course that would solve the problem for us in one way, wouldn't it, Aaron?"

"Not the best way."

"No, not the best way. Not the ideal solution. Not *my* first choice, certainly. Still, you have to look on the bright side of everything. We wouldn't need to worry about crossing that bridge any more, and that's one thing."

"Why don't you go back and find another way?" asked Rose, looking over at the stairs.

"You're welcome to try, certainly. Most of us have tried, once or twice. We found that when we went up the stairs, we somehow ended up coming right back down the stairs, and here we are again. Still, you might have more luck."

"And how do you know," said Rose, "that *his* gun is loaded?"

"That's another excellent question. Don't you think that's an excellent question, Aaron?"

But Aaron must have either tired abruptly of the game, or else taken offense for some inscrutable reason, for he muttered, "Fuck off," in a low voice and stared down at his feet in broody silence.

"The answer," said Michael, "is that of course we don't. In fact—and I'm telling you this in confidence, just between you, me and the young gentleman's overcoat—the fact is, that I think there's a very good chance that gun *isn't* loaded at all, and we've all been sitting here stuck for days and no good reason in the world. Which is enough to make a fellow feel like crying, or laughing, or laughing and then crying. But unfortunately, you see, there's only one way to find out for sure, and no one wants to be the one who's standing there on the bridge with that wee shotgun pointing at him, and the fellow pulls the trigger and the hammer comes down and we all get to know."

Rose began looking around the wharf, trying to think of some other way out of there. Below her feet, the blood from the stairs poured steadily between the rotting boards and into the river. Certainly they could never swim across, even the strongest swimmer would get snatched away by the current like a pine cone, and of course Emmanuel couldn't swim at all. Even if they made it across to the other side, there didn't seem to be any way to climb back out. They couldn't drown, they were already dead, but they might very well get stuck in there forever. She briefly, ludicrously, imagined them all trying to build a boat; pulling down wood from the buildings around them and jury-rigging some kind of raft.

Still, she thought, if they couldn't get across the river and they couldn't go back by the stairs, perhaps they could go *through* the houses, or even over them. There were more than enough people here. They could knock a hole in the wall or knock down a door, or figure a way to get someone up to one of the second-storey windows. For all they knew, this really *was* the centre; maybe the queen was even somewhere inside these very buildings. And if it wasn't, and if that didn't lead them anywhere, if it only brought them back to this landing like the stairs apparently did, they could try going over the rooftops, they looked flat enough to scramble across. Anything would be better than just sitting here waiting.

She began looking around at the people gathered there to see if any of them had some rope, or anything else that might be useful, when she realized that a number of them had gotten to their feet, that everyone was staring intently and silently, even eagerly, at the bridge, and that Emmanuel was no longer standing at her side.

She pushed her way forward. Emmanuel had started across the bridge, which swayed and shook in the wind. She called out to him, told him to come back, but when he heard her voice he just pushed forward, as though afraid that if he paused at all he might lose his nerve completely.

He called back to her, saying something like, "Don't worry," but his voice was drowned and twisted in the wind and she couldn't make it out for certain. The man in the middle was pointing the shotgun at him, swaying drunkenly, the blood pulsing from his neck and streaming from his head. A single livid eyeball was visible in the wreckage, impossibly large. There was a sort of mouth there as well, a red hole with a few broken teeth and bits of bone showing, but hardly any other trace of a human face. The man put both hands on the gun now to hold it steady, leaning his body against the ropes of the bridge, and he covered the trigger with one finger.

Rose stood at the mouth of the bridge, terrified and uncertain. She was afraid that if she tried running out after Emmanuel it might frighten the man even more, scare him into pulling that trigger. She tried calling out again, urging Emmanuel to come back, telling him she had a better idea, but she wasn't even sure that he could hear her over the wind. She was vaguely aware that Aaron and Michael were standing right behind her now, almost touching her, but all her focus was on her friend.

Emmanuel continued to inch closer to the man, inch by agonizingly slow inch. When he got within seven or eight feet, the man let out a hideous, unearthly kind of cry that echoed across the canal. And when Emmanuel got within four or five feet of him, close enough that he could have stretched out his arm and touched the tip of the gun with his finger, and everyone on either side of the bridge held their breath and stood frozen, motionless, in pained excited silence, the man pulled the trigger. The hammer fell and nothing happened, just a hollow empty click. He had no ammunition.

Emmanuel's legs seemed to give out beneath him, in the immensity of relief, and he had to grab the rope for support. Rose felt a surge of relief, and of happy anger, and started onto the bridge. Once they were safely across, she planned to yell at Emmanuel for his idiotic heroics and scaring the hell out of her. And then so many things began happening at once.

The man, having failed to shoot Emmanuel, lifted the shotgun over his head with both hands, like an axe, and chopped down at the boy. At the same time, there was a roar of inchoate voices, and several people from the opposite landing rushed out onto the bridge, making it sway and jump wildly. The man missed Emmanuel's head, catching just a glancing blow off his shoulder as the leaping bridge caused him to lurch wildly. The shotgun leapt out of his hand, skittered off the planks, and dropped into the river below, disappearing beneath the blood. Emmanuel nearly followed it, falling and sprawling down. The lower half of his body hung off the side of the bridge, dangling in the air, and he clung desperately to the planks, digging his fingernails into the rotting wood. Rose started running forward to help him, but she got no more than a few steps when Aaron put his hand roughly on her shoulder and pushed her aside, against the ropes, wrenching the stick from her hand as he bullied his way past her. And his face was congested and swollen and his eyes glazed over.

One of the men from the far side had reached the middle now, and swung his fist into the man's pulpy head with a spatter of blood and a soft nauseating squish. Then Aaron was there from the other side, stepping on Emmanuel's hand as he drove the stick, spear-like, into the man's belly. The bridge was shaking and jumping manically as more people rushed on from either side. Rose saw Emmanuel lose his grip and slip, and disappear from her sight, and then she was falling, too, and so was everybody else, a confused kaleidoscopic chaos of flailing bodies and pirouetting boards and undulating ropes as the bridge snapped and disintegrated beneath the weight. And then she was plunged under the hot rolling blood, and all she could see was red.

Rose plunged in headfirst, and for a long time she wasn't even sure which way was up. The salty, hot blood stung her eyes blind and rushed into her nose and mouth. She swallowed some, rusty and putrid, and her stomach instantly rebelled, cramping and spasming painfully, vomiting blood and bile up into her mouth, and her throat tore up and burned. Her fingers and toes and nose all swelled and crackled with pain, the blood scalding against her frozen skin, and by the time she finally found the surface, her lungs were screaming for relief, they felt like they would explode. She gulped in the air and spat the blood and vomit from her mouth as she was spun and tossed by the current like a rag doll, but the blood was still in her eyes and her blood-soaked hair was plastered over her eyes and she could see nothing, she could hear nothing but the rush and the blood pounding in her ears and wild, distorted howls; she tried yelling out Emmanuel's name and she could hardly even hear herself. She couldn't wipe her eyes, it was all she could do to keep her head bobbing and straining above the surface, and she was swept blindly down the canal.

# 13

I DIDN'T HAVE A PARTY OR ANYTHING FOR MY FOURTEENTH birthday. I didn't really want one anyway. They took me out for lunch, we went for dim sum so that Mom could have those fried shrimp cakes and shark-fin dumplings.

Because my birthday falls on Remembrance Day I never have school, which is pretty awesome, but Davey had to go to work anyway, so it was going to be just me and Jack and Mom, only when we got to the restaurant it turned out that Davey had lied, he didn't have to work, he'd booked the day off for me, and he was there with Tante Martìne and Conrad, too.

Tante Martìne spent most of lunch telling Davey to tell his wife what she should or shouldn't eat. She always referred to Mom as his wife, after she found out about the baby, though whether it was out of senility or sarcasm I could never quite decide. And if Davey was around, she'd usually avoid talking directly to her, and would talk through Davey instead, poking him in the arm and saying, Davey, Davey, tell your wife this, or tell your wife that. She was big on poking people. At my birthday lunch she drank two beer and wouldn't eat anything but the pork buns, and those she covered with so much hot sauce I don't know how she even tasted them.

After lunch we all went back to the house, and there was cake and presents and stuff, and Davey made pizza for dinner and Conrad stayed the whole night and hung out the next morning, so it was a pretty decent birthday after all. I remember Conrad gave me a really odd gift, it was a little glass ballerina with pink slippers on a platform, arms up above the head, and when you wound the key she turned slow circles to a tinny clockwork tune. The music was supposed to be from the Nutcracker but it wasn't very musical. He waited until the morning to give it to me, when Mom and Davey and Jack were all still upstairs in bed, so that was a little odd too, I thought. But sweet.

Even Tante Martìne had a present for me, a kind of weird woolly toque with ear flaps that she must have knit out of leftover wool because it was black, brown and a small bit of purple with no discernable pattern to the colours at all. When Addy came over for Christmas I loaned it to her and she wore it the whole time she was here. I would have let her take it back to Montreal with her, she liked it so much she even offered to swap her Expos cap for it, but you know it's bad luck to trade away a gift.

It was around this time that Casey and Addy got the news that Addy's grandmother had passed away, finally for real. She told me over the same phone conversation when I was telling her about my birthday, and the present Conrad gave me and stuff, and she cut me off, all excited, and said, "Oh, oh, that reminds me!" I can't imagine why a little glass ballerina could have reminded her of her grandmother dying, but whatever.

They had received this registered letter, from a lawyer or the coroner or something, Casey had to sign for it and everything. It said that the old woman had died in Niagara Falls, in a cheap motel on the American side. She'd been staying at the motel for almost a week when she passed away in her sleep. The chambermaid found her in the morning, lying on top of the blankets, pale and peaceful and completely naked, her red and grey hair unbraided and spread out in a great fan like a peacock's tail, covering the whole bed almost. That's what Addy told me over the phone, but she must have been making that up, cause why would they put that kind of detail in a lawyer's letter?

So Casey had to go to Niagara, to identify the body and sign papers, stuff like that. Addy desperately wanted to go with her, of course, but Casey absolutely refused. And when Addy tried to press her on it, she said, "Okay, I'll tell you what, you get a refund on those plane tickets to Winnipeg, you can buy your own bus ticket to Niagara."

When Addy told me that, for a moment I was terrified. It would have been so like her to say yes, to call her mom on her bluff and do exactly that—partly just for the sake of not letting her mom get her way, partly because I knew how much she must have wanted to go. I mean, she'd never been to Niagara or even crossed the US border before, but she'd spent half her life here in Winnipeg. I would have been devastated if she didn't come, but I don't think that would have ever occurred to her, and of course I never would have said anything.

But for whatever reason, she didn't do it. Maybe the tickets turned out to be non-refundable, maybe she just decided that seeing a baby get born would be more interesting than a dead grandma in Niagara. I don't know, I didn't ask. Casey went on her own and left Addy alone in their apartment with a leftover chicken, four cans of ravioli, and twenty dollars "for emergencies," which I think Addy used to go see a movie.

We talked on the phone a few times that weekend, when her mom was away. I asked her if Casey had called from Niagara to tell her she'd arrived safe and if there was any news or anything, and Addy said, "No, of course not. She probably won't tell me anything when she comes home, either."

And then we started imagining what Addy would do if Casey never came back at all. We didn't know yet about the RV being sold, and we assumed that Casey would inherit it. We didn't know if there was a will or anything either, or whether there was any money left to inherit, but Casey was the only next-of-kin, she had no brothers or sisters, no aunts and uncles still living. So we imagined Casey taking over the RV, and instead of coming back to Montreal, just driving away, and one day Addy would get a newspaper clipping in the mail of her mom's first obituary, saying she had invented the electric toothbrush and was killed in a freak skydiving accident over Mount Rushmore.

"Maybe it's like a curse," Addy said dreamily. "Like a Flying Dutchman kind of thing. And then one day when Mom finally dies,

I'll inherit the RV from her and I'll be forced to wander the continent forever, faking my death in every city. That would be awesome. Only then *I'd* have to have a daughter to send the obits to and stuff, so forget that." Addy had always insisted she was never going to get married or have kids, whenever we used to fantasize about our futures.

"Maybe that'll be how you break the curse," I said, "If you don't have a daughter to pass it on to."

"I guess that could work," she said pensively. "And then the curse would die with me, right? But I'd have to have *someone* to send the obits to, it would be way too pathetic if you went and put them in the papers but you didn't have anyone to actually read them."

"You could send them to me. We could work out a secret code, so I'd read them and know what you were really up to—like if you said that you were a llama farmer and you died in a tractor accident, I'd know it actually meant you were living on a houseboat in Florida or something."

"That could work," she said. "I always wanted to live on a houseboat. Kinda sounds like cheating, though, I'll have to think about it."

Of course I told Addy that if Casey never came back from Niagara, she could just come and live with us. She already had the ticket to Winnipeg, she'd just have to figure out how to survive until Christmas, or she could try and cash it in for a one-way ticket that left sooner. Mom would bitch and complain, but she wouldn't say no, not in the end. Whatever she might say, I knew that deep down she thought of Addy as almost a daughter.

Addy agreed, but I didn't think she sounded very enthusiastic about it. I think she felt that if her mom ever really did something as awesome as abandon her to roam the continent under a curse, she'd want to do something a lot more fun and romantic than just come live with *us* again. Like she could busk her way across the country, because she'd have Casey's guitar and no one to tell her she couldn't play. "Or I could hitchhike to LA," she said cheerfully, "and get discovered or something."

But of course Casey did come home the next day, just like she was supposed to. She wouldn't tell Addy much, only that it really was her grandma, and she really was actually dead at last. Casey had told them to cremate the body and toss the ashes in the trash and there wasn't going to be a funeral, and no, there was no cursed and doomed RV to inherit, the RV had been sold a year ago. She brought home two big suitcases stuffed with old lady clothes and notebooks, and she locked them in the storage closet in the basement of their apartment block and she said that was it, that's all there was to inherit, but Addy had her suspicions.

She said they ought to write a real obituary for her now, but Casey said no way, forget it. I guess she still hadn't forgiven her mother. Addy went and wrote one anyway, and put it in the *Montreal Gazette* with her own money. She clipped it out and sent it to me. Mostly it was merely true, like where she was born, who she married, where and how she died. Addy had to keep it fairly short because she couldn't afford to put in the long elaborate one she'd written, but she did slip in one made-up detail, about her grandma giving birth to an illegitimate son named Felipé Pelícano San Cristobal Jimenez in the bathroom of a Tijuana taqueria. She was pretty proud of that. "I think Grandma would have really appreciated it," she said to me.

Around the end of November, it got so cold one night our pipes burst. No one could take a shower or a bath for four days until the landlord finally came over and he and Davey replaced them.

They had to punch three big holes in the walls to get at the pipes: one in the bathroom, behind the tub; one in the laundry room down in the basement, where the drywall was soaked through for shit anyway; and one in my room, a hole in the wall about a foot and a half square, just above my bed. The landlord said he'd come back that weekend and fix the walls, but we didn't hear from him again until almost the spring. Whenever I lay in bed, if someone was in the bathroom I could hear exactly what they were doing, just like I was in the same room. It was disgusting.

By this time Mom was already home off work. She'd been hoping to work right up until Christmas but it was just too hard, being on her feet all day, the veins were popping out of her legs and her back was killing her. The doctor was worried about her blood pressure too. And then the cold—just that short trip to work and back was too much, the cold was so brutal. So she was practically a prisoner in the house, restless, heavy and unhappy, puking, blotchy, sleepless, bored, unbeautiful and embarrassed. Davey had to start working extra hours, putting in overtime every night, to help make up for the money they were missing from Mom's tips.

It was hard having her around the house all the time, especially those three or four hours after school, Jack and I were used to doing whatever we wanted. I remember thinking how small the house seemed those last couple months with Mom home, and the cold so you didn't want to go outside ever, everyone tripping all over one another and snapping at each other. And pretty soon the baby was going to be here and the house would seem even smaller, I couldn't imagine how we were going to stand it.

It was so cold that Conrad stopped coming over in the mornings, and Davey would drive me and Jack both to school. Then we wouldn't see Davey until ten, maybe ten-thirty or eleven at night when he'd come home too exhausted to talk anyway. And I'd have to come home straight after school, because Mom would be there waiting and watching the clock to make sure I did. It was probably too cold to want to walk over to the high school and hang out, even if she wasn't.

The worst part was that the more pregnant Mom got, the more we had to put up with Tante Martìne coming around. She had her own car, a big boat of an old Pontiac, and it was always terrifying to see her drive it, with her wrinkly little scrunched-up bran-muffin-brown face barely peeking over the steering wheel, big eyes blinking like a hummingbird's wings. By the time November ended and then we were into December, and Mom was trapped in the house like a shut-in, Tante Martìne would drop by two or three times a week, when Davey was at work and me and Jack were at school, and she'd clean the house and order Mom around. She was always telling Mom what to eat and what not to eat, how to sit, when to lie down. She made great pots of greasy soup with mysterious foreign objects floating around in them, Jack and Davey loved them but Mom and I couldn't eat them at all. She tried to ban all salad from the house, cause she said leafy greens would make the baby gassy, which gave me this weird unpleasant image of the fetus farting away inside my mother's stomach. She also tried to convince Mom to drink this weird twiggy tea all the time. When I got home from school I always knew if Tante Martìne had been there because the house would reek of that tea, it smelled like toadstools on a rotting tree stump. I wondered if she had been a midwife or something back in Trinidad, but Davey said no, not as far as he knew.

At least she didn't come to the hospital the day Mom went into labour. That would have been way too much. I think Mom must have made Davey swear on his life that he absolutely wouldn't call Tante Martìne and tell her anything until after it was all over, and Mom and the baby were home and safe and had a chance to at least sleep a little.

At first Mom hadn't even wanted *us* to come to the hospital with them, after all the work we did to dig out her car. She said we should just wait at home and they'd call us when it was all over, which started a big argument, because like I said to her, Addy had sold her hair just so she could come all the way from Montreal for this, and Addy said cheerfully, "That's all right. Go on, drive away without us, Nat and I'll just walk to the hospital. We'll probably get lost in the blizzard and freeze to death, and then you'll feel silly."

Davey said, "For God's sake let them come if they want to come, let's just get in the car and go."

Jack, who was standing over the heating vent and holding his hands in his armpits to try and thaw them out, said, "*I'll* stay home, I don't mind." There were flecks of blood on his lip where the cold had cracked it back open.

"The hell you will," said Davey. "Get in the car, we're all going."

Jack said, "What? Why me?"

And Davey said, "Because we're a family, that's why, and we're all in this together, and if we get stuck on the way I'll need your help to push us out, now get in the goddamn car."

# 14

ROSE HAD NO IDEA HOW LONG SHE WAS IN THE RIVER. BY THE time she got her eyes cleared and could see, Emmanuel was nowhere in sight, nor anyone else who had been on the bridge with them, only her alone and a handful of debris.

A black despair and hopelessness washed over her: she had lost her only friend, she was being swept away from the centre of the city and her sister, and she might never be able to get out of here, she might be stuck in this river forever, half-drowning in perpetual pain and misery.

Presently the canal grew wider, and the wind must have slackened, for the surface became less wavy and choppy though the current pulled her along just as quickly. Rose began swimming towards the nearest wall—more out of boredom, perhaps, tired of doing nothing and being swept passively downstream, than out of any renewed sense of hope or determination. Rose had always been a strong swimmer, and though her arms were weak from treading blood and her whole body bristled with pain, she eventually reached the edge.

The buildings lining the walls of the canal presented the exact same face as they had by the bridge, identical on either side, but as the river widened, so had the walls grown higher. They were made of wooden planks, nailed vertically to the cut steep banks and soft and rotten with age. Rose found she could push her fingers right into the wood, but when she tried to hold on, she only came away with a fistful of pulpy splinters, and the current kept dragging her along, every bit as strong here as it had been out in the middle of the river. Even if she had managed to stop herself from moving, there would have been nothing to grab on to, no possible way to pull herself up the fifteen or twenty feet to the level of the houses. She wondered, now, where the river could be taking her. If it did go to the outskirts of the city it couldn't possibly go beyond the outskirts, for there was no beyond. Which meant, she reasoned, that the river either had to end somewhere, or it simply went around in a great unending circle. And if it went around in a great unending circle, then sooner or later it would come back again to the place where she had fallen in. The wharf would be there, and she could get beneath it, catch on to the piles. The remnants of the bridge must be there too, ropes and planks dangling down in the rushing blood, and people, perhaps, standing on the wharf and looking for a way forward, people who could help pull her out. She had only to stay close to the wall and let the current carry her along, and sooner or later it would come around. It must. It had to. She might even see Emmanuel again.

So she drifted along, always watching the opposite side of the canal, as far ahead as she could see. She knew that when—and if—the wharf reappeared, it would probably do so suddenly, seemingly out of nowhere, just as the intersections in the streets always appeared. But it worried her a little that the canal seemed to only continue getting gradually but steadily wider and deeper, and even though the waves had died down completely and the current now slackened a little, making it far less tiring to keep her head above the surface, it made her wonder if maybe her guess was wrong, and it wouldn't come back around after all.

Then, up ahead, she saw something she would never have expected: a tiny island in the middle of the river, perhaps twenty or thirty feet across, choked with trees and undergrowth, and a lone black tower rising out of the centre, high into the sky. Without hesitation, without even thinking, Rose pushed away from the side of the canal and swam towards it with long strong frantic strokes, a burst of energy born of desperation, terrified lest the current sweep her past before she could reach it.

The current pushed her into a small inlet, where the surface of the blood was covered with pink and scummy foam and choked with thin and tangling hair-like weeds, and debris that bobbed up and down and back and forth. Rose unthinkingly grabbed hold of what she thought was a tree branch, and was horrified to find that she was holding on to a bone, long and heavy like someone's thigh, and with bits of tendon and raw flesh still clinging to it.

The top of the bank was only a couple feet above the level of the river, but it took Rose a long time to haul herself up by the overhanging grass and weeds, and then scramble on to the dry bank. Finally free of the river of blood, she lay there a long time on her back in the grass, crying helplessly, just like when she had first arrived in the city.

When she was all cried out, she got to her feet, still dripping blood, to look around. The undergrowth here was the same as everywhere in the city—weeds and grass, thistles and brambles, briar and burdock—but the trees were Scotch pines and squat and twisty crabapple trees, thick and ripe with fruit that fell in slimy little piles, and blue and yellow flowers peeked out among the weeds and grass, and the whole place smelled of sweet, rotting apples and pine needles, a sweet relief after months and months of smelling nothing but death. The sight and smell of the apples made her hunger pangs even sharper, but though Rose knew she couldn't eat them and it was a kind of torture to be near them, yet it was a kind of pleasure also. Perhaps best of all, there was no wind here, not the slightest breeze, and without it the kind of peaceful and complete silence that she had almost forgotten about, and that reminded her of the still and soundless arctic nights from when she was a child, when it was so cold that even sounds seemed to freeze.

Above the treetops, she could see the spire of the thin black tower, rising a hundred feet or more, and she started to make her way carefully towards it. She could see only a single window, a narrow one at the very top, just below the level of the roof. The island, now that she was on it, proved to be much larger than it had appeared from the river. The pine needles that carpeted the ground were sharp as pins, and the burrs and thorns and thistles tugged and grabbed at her. Rose had to make her way very carefully, watching where she stepped, and here and there she saw more bones, white and red, poking out from beneath the rotting fruit and the snarled and choking weeds.

She came at last to a small clearing where there was only grass, and in the middle of the clearing, the base of the tower. It was black marble, smooth and perfect and cool to the touch, and no matter how many times she circled it—it was hardly wider around than an elevator shaft—she couldn't see any possible way in, only that single window at the very top. Nor was there any crack or crevice or the faintest hope of climbing, not even a monkey or a squirrel could have done it. She stood there for a while, staring up at the window and wondering what it might mean, wondering too if she might catch a glimpse of someone moving around. She tried calling out, yelling up, but her voice seemed distant and faint even to her own ears, and there was no sign of any response.

Rose decided to explore the island further, and then come back and try again. As she was circling the edge of the clearing, trying to remember which direction she had come from, she heard a voice in the distance—faintly, it almost sounded like someone singing, or trying to sing. It seemed to be coming from the far side of the island, and Rose followed it through the trees. As she got closer, she could hear the voice more clearly, though she couldn't quite make out any words or what language they might be in, but it was a girl's voice for certain, and a cheerful gentle tune. And then she came to the edge of the forest, at a place where a number of large grey and white rocks overhung the river, and a young woman perched on the farthest outcropping, her back to Rose, long, thick, curly, red-brown hair tumbling all the way down her back and across the rocks. Rose couldn't see her face, but she immediately noticed the shadow that fell behind her, and she could see that the girl had a half-eaten apple in one hand, and Rose knew that this must be the queen. As she watched, standing only ten feet away, the girl took two quick bites of the crabapple, tossed the core into the river, and skipped lightly to her feet, turning around. Her shadow turned with her, so that wherever she faced, it always fell behind her.

She looked to be about the same age as Rose, perhaps fifteen or sixteen years old. She wore a plain white T-shirt that came down almost to her knees, and nothing else; the shirt had blood and mud stains on it, but they were faded and dry, as though it had somehow been washed. And the girl's arms and legs looked clean and fresh, too, without any cuts or scrapes or bruises; her fingernails were long and clear, tapered to delicate points. But when Rose saw the queen's face, she got a tremendous shock, and she blurted out, "Oh my God—Addy, is that you?"

For the queen looked exactly like a girl Rose used to know from school: she had the same round and freckled face, the same lithe and boyish body, the same beautiful long red-brown hair hanging down her back. She had the same big green eyes, two slightly different colours, the right one that kind of hazel colour people call green but it really isn't, and the left one green for real, green as an emerald or a blade of grass. But it *couldn't* be Addy, for it had to be the queen, eating and casting a shadow, and the queen had been here since before she was born, while Addy—as far as Rose knew—Addy was still alive.

"La, of course it's me," the girl said cheerfully. "Who are you and what's an Addy?" Her voice, at least, was definitely different than Addy's was. She spoke with a kind of chipper lilt, and a mercurial, shifty, unplaceable accent.

Rose blushed, and felt confused. "Addy is... I'm sorry, it's just a girl I used to know, when I was alive. You look so much like her."

"Really?" said the queen, delighted. "I've never been told I look like anyone before. No one tells me anything," she added, suddenly sounding aggrieved and irritated, and narrowing her eyes.

"Are you— You're the queen, aren't you?" Rose wondered if she ought to be bowing, or curtsying, or calling her "Your Majesty."

"Yes, yes, of course I am, everybody tells me *that*," she complained. "They tell me I'm the queen all the time, but do they ever tell me anything useful? Do they ever tell me anything interesting?

It's a conspiracy, la. Oh well," she said, abruptly cheerful again, "I'll just refuse to set them free, that'll teach 'em. What's your name? You smell disgusting."

"Rose. I'm sorry."

"Why are you sorry? I've heard much worse names, at least yours is short."

From the direction of the tower, the girls heard the sound of someone making his way through the brush, and a man's voice calling out, "Your Majesty? Your Majesty?"

"Oh, *la*," said the queen. "That must be Sebastian. He's probably coming to tell me I'm the queen, in case I've forgotten since he told me half an hour ago. Don't tell him you saw me," she said in a loud, stagey and conspiratorial whisper as she skipped dexterously across the rocks. "And tell him I said to give you a bath." And then she was gone, seeming to just disappear, so that Rose couldn't even say for sure what direction she'd disappeared in.

# 15

OF COURSE WE WEREN'T ALLOWED TO GO INTO THE ACTUAL birthing room with Mom and Davey and the doctor, we had to just sit in the waiting room for six or seven hours, wondering.

Jack complained the whole time we were there. He complained because he was hungry, he complained because he was bored, he complained because his lip hurt and his nose and fingers were frostbit and his arms and shoulders were aching. He complained because the plastic seats were making his butt numb, because the place smelled like a hospital, and because there weren't even any cute nurses around he could pass the time checking out. There was a TV mounted up in the waiting room but he couldn't find anything decent to watch except a stupid soccer game, so he complained about that too.

I kind of think that he complained so much to cover the fact that he was anxious and worried—worried whether Mom and the baby were going to be okay. I know I was, although hunger and worry can be hard to tell apart sometimes, they both make my stomach cramp up. I mean, there was no real reason to think that they *wouldn't* be okay, but you never know, and I just couldn't understand why it was taking so long. It probably didn't help Jack that Addy really had done a lot of research, and filled the time by chatting happily to us and in very vivid detail about breech births, episiotomies and anal fissures, prolapsed uteruses and exploding placentas and caesarian sections, but I found it strangely comforting—just the fact that Addy was there with us, where she belonged, being Addy.

Every time a door was opened, the sound of someone in pain would drift through the corridors and into the waiting room, mingling with the echoey footsteps and creaky wheels going up and down the linoleum floors. There were other women in labour all around. One woman walked up and down the corridors and in and out of the waiting room and the bathroom the whole time we were there. They had her attached to one of those IV drips that she wheeled around with her, sometimes crying softly, sometimes snapping violently at her poor husband if he tried to touch her or tell her it would be all right.

There was another woman, a really young looking one, who arrived while we were there. They took a poke at her and then turned her away, said she wasn't really in labour and told her to go home. I felt so bad for her, she and her boyfriend barely looked older than Jack and Addy, and then to make her go back out into that brutal storm, the snow and the cold, seemed like such a mean thing to do. It didn't even seem like it ought to be legal, like if anything bad happened to them it ought to be murder.

It had taken over an hour just to get to the hospital, for what normally should have been maybe a five or ten minute drive. Davey and Jack had to get out and push twice before we even got to Main Street. Then Addy would sit behind the wheel and work the gas as they were pushing, and Mom in the back seat with me, squeezing my hand so hard I thought she was going to crush some bones. There was no one else on the streets, the whole city seemed abandoned, and it was still dark as night out almost even though the sun must have been up by then.

Addy spent the whole trip loudly timing the length of Mom's contractions, and the time between her contractions, and trying to coach Mom about her breathing, and Mom spent pretty much the whole trip saying, "Shut up, Addy," which of course didn't faze Addy at all. At one point she asked Mom if she could check to see how dilated she was, and Mom threatened to kick her out of the car and just abandon her out on the street. I think she was almost serious too.

It wasn't until after we got to the hospital, and we got checked in and they hustled Mom and Davey away and left us behind in the waiting room without a word, that it occurred to us that we hadn't really eaten anything, and we were all starving. Jack had made that great big breakfast but once Mom's water broke we all forgot to eat it, it was just sitting there in the kitchen, congealing. And we didn't have any money either. All we could come up with between us was a buck and a half in loose change, enough to get one chocolate bar and split it three ways, which if anything just made me feel hungrier after I'd eaten it.

Jack thought we should ask one of the nurses to go in, find Davey, and pry his wallet out of him so we could go down to the cafeteria and buy some lunch. But none of the nurses would pay any attention to us when we tried to flag them down or talk to them. They would just give us a quick, nasty glance and hustle by. I think they must have been short-staffed because of the blizzard. There weren't as many nurses around as you'd expect and the ones we did see all looked totally stressed out and harassed. The one at the front desk would stare over at us occasionally with this evil suspicious glare like we were a pack of criminals, like she expected us to try and make off with some bottles of hand sanitizer or something. It was true that with Jack's lip all cracked open and bleeding, and the bloody Kleenex shoved up Addy's nose, we did look pretty rough.

Addy offered to go look for Davey herself. "Why bother the nurses? I'll just slip in and find him myself, no big deal, no one'll even notice." But Jack and I both said no way in hell. She'd either end up getting us all kicked out of the maternity ward, or she'd end up in a hospital gown, mask and gloves, helping deliver somebody's baby, and Jack and I would be left by ourselves in the waiting room, still bored and starving to death.

So then she suggested that we go down to the emergency ward and check in as patients. She figured we could just leave our coats and stuff behind and stand outside for ten minutes, maybe roll around in a snowbank a bit, and then say we'd been out all night and ask to get treated for hypothermia, frostbite and starvation— the idea being that if we were actual patients, they'd be bound to feed us something. What do they give someone who has hypothermia? Probably chicken noodle soup or something. I could have gone for some chicken noodle soup.

By that time I was so hungry I was almost tempted to give it a try, but the thing was, what if we left the maternity ward and Davey came to the waiting room as soon as we were gone, come to tell us it was all over and the baby was born? We seriously expected him to appear any moment, the entire time that we were there. The way Mom had been carrying on in the car and from what Addy was saying about her contractions, I had figured we were lucky to even get her checked in at the hospital before the kid popped out. So all we could do was sit there and wait, and wait, and hour after hour trickled by, unbelievably slow.

When Davey finally came and fetched us, he told us it was "all over except for the crying," and you could tell he'd been crying too, his eyes were all swollen and red and his face was blotchy and grey, he looked like a used-up oil rag, but he also looked absolutely happy, and I remember feeling at that moment glad for my little sister that Davey was going to make such a good father for her, which was weird, because it wasn't something that I'd thought about before.

Jack asked if everybody was okay, and Davey said, "Fine, fine, everybody's fine, all healthy, A-okay."

Addy asked what the baby was like, and Davey said, "It's a girl!" triumphantly, as if this was surprising and exciting news.

"Well, we know *that*," said Addy impatiently. "How big is she? Does she have hair? How many fingers and toes? Vestigial tail?"

"She's tiny," he said. "Six pounds, eleven ounces. Looks like a greasy, little, wrinkled otter. Lots of hair." And then he said, "Come on, come see for yourself."

But they wouldn't let us go in right away, we had to wait another twenty minutes before they led us to a room on the far side of the ward. It was one of those shared rooms with a curtain cutting it in half. Mom had the bed closest to the door, and on the other side of the curtain we could hear a woman sobbing ferociously the entire time we were there, and her poor husband trying to comfort her, sounding frightened, small, confused and useless.

Mom was sitting up in bed, cradling the baby and crying gently and happily, she looked like complete shit but she also looked beautiful at the same time, if that makes any sense. She passed the baby to Davey for a minute so we could all look at her, and she was beautiful too, even though her face was kind of squashed and her skin was all wrinkly, which actually made her look a little bit like Tante Martìne, poor thing. She had a little cap of patchy black curly hair on the crown of her head, and she also had tiny little hairs all over her cheeks and neck and body, which Addy pointed out to me. "Like a little baby wolf-man," she squealed.

"They'll fall out," Mom said. "Give me back my baby. It's perfectly normal. You had little hairs all over you too."

The poor little thing was starting to mewl and fuss and cry, so Mom lifted her shirt and stuck her face on her nipple. Jack blushed bright red and said, "Oh, God," turning his face and holding his hand over his eyes, and Mom said, "Oh, grow up."

"Well," said Addy, "I think she looks like a Lucy."

That wasn't a name I'd really considered, but I kind of liked it. Lucy. "Lucy's a nice name," I said timidly.

"Definitely a Lucy," Addy said again, in a that-settles-that sort of voice. "Just look at her."

"She already has a name," Mom said. I knew it. And with a hint of defensiveness, she told us at last: "Her name is Madeline."

There was a brief, shocked silence.

"Hey!" said Addy indignantly. "That's *my* name." She always did say that she ought to have been named Madeline, not her sister.

"No," said Mom, "it's *my* name, that's what I was going to name Jack before I knew he was a boy, and your mother stole it from me." She narrowed her eyes, obviously brooding on an old, old grievance. Davey, who I don't know if he'd ever heard about Addy's twin dead sister even, just looked thoroughly confused.

"I don't know," said Jack. "That's a little creepy, isn't it?"

"It's been sixteen years, dammit. I couldn't use it for Natalie, but I'm taking it back now. My little Madeline, just like the stories." And looking down at the baby in her arms, sucking greedily at her breast, she started to recite from memory: "She was not afraid of mice, she loved winter, snow and ice. To the tigers in the zoo, Madeline just said, 'Poo-poo.'"

"See?" said Addy. "That's just like me, *I'm* not afraid of mice, I *knew* it should have been my name."

"Well, now it's *her* name," Mom said. "So suck it up."

"What about her middle name?" I asked. "That could be Lucy, couldn't it?"

"No, sweetie, I'm sorry. Her middle name is going to be Martina. Madeline Martina Toussaint."

Davey gave a little whoop and holler of triumph, whether because of the last name or the middle one I'm not sure. Jack took Davey's wallet and came back forty minutes later with three huge bags of Taco Bell, and we all feasted on it there in the room, even Mom, until a nurse came in and yelled at us.

We got home around midnight that night, after visiting hours were long over and they finally threatened to call security. Mom and the baby were supposed be coming home tomorrow afternoon if everything was okay.

The storm had finally let up, but enough more snow had fallen that Davey only got the car halfway into the drive before it got stuck. He spun the wheels for a minute, and then got Jack to help him push it a foot or two further in, just so it wasn't completely blocking the back lane, and then left it there, saying, "Screw it, we'll dig it out in the morning."

The kitchen was a disaster. Breakfast was still sitting out on the stovetop where Jack had cooked it, except for the bacon. Typhus had apparently gotten into the bacon, knocking the frying pan to the floor and spattering congealed grease all over the place, it was so disgusting I almost puked.

Poor Jack had to clean it up, cause after all it was his cat. Addy offered to lend him a hand—she was the only one of us who didn't look dead on her feet. She didn't look tired at all. Davey took a beer out of the fridge and the phone and went upstairs, and I went straight to bed. I didn't even get changed, just took off my jeans and got under the covers.

As soon as I closed my eyes, I started to cry, I don't know why— I guess maybe just all the excitement and nervous tension, but I was really sobbing for a few minutes, and then I was kind of half-sobbing, half-laughing because it seemed so ridiculous and stupid that I was crying, and I was glad that Addy hadn't come to bed yet, and then I was asleep.

# 16

NO SOONER HAD THE QUEEN SKIPPED AWAY AND DISAPPEARED than a man emerged from the trees, further along up the bank. He was a darkish man, perhaps in his thirties, with olive skin and a wispy, brief goatee on a flat but not unattractive face. He was thin and fit and there was a blood-red rag bound around his throat.

Like the queen, his arms and face were clean, and so were his clothes, more or less. But unlike her, he was definitely dead himself, with bruises and scrapes all over his body, and the worn, weary, sick and famished look that all the dead possessed. He saw Rose, and for a moment his eyes glazed over with some dark, indecipherable expression, then he forced himself to smile, and bowed slightly. "Español?" he asked. "Deutsch? English?"

"Yes," said Rose, "English."

"Are you a pilgrim?"

"Yes," said Rose. "I suppose I am."

"You must have just arrived. Have you seen a young lady about, with long red hair?"

She hesitated, and then shook her head no. He frowned, and looked thoughtfully down the river, flowing into the distance. Then he shrugged, and said, "Come with me. We should get you cleaned up, before the queen sees you."

He led her up the bank a little ways, back in the direction he'd come from, to an open spot where the outcropping rocks were dripping with blood and the ground was spongy with blood and smelled like death. Three crude canoes or kayaks were tethered to the rocks, bobbing on the surface of the blood, and here a path penetrated into the woods, beaten and flattened in through the brush and the briar, leading back to the tower.

As he led her along, Sebastian plucked a dozen or so crabapples, putting them into a small sack that appeared to have been fashioned out of an old shirt or gown. When they reached the tower, he went and stood beneath the window and knocked on the wall five times, in a little rhythmic pattern. Then he stood back and patiently looked up at the window. It took some time, but presently Rose saw a head appear in the window, peer down, and then disappear again, followed by a rope ladder that rattled down the hundred feet or more to the ground.

Sebastian gestured graciously at the ladder. "Please," he said, and Rose stepped forward, hesitantly. The rungs of the ladder were bones, and the ropes that strung them together were made of human hair, all different shades, carefully braided and bound.

"It's quite strong, I promise," Sebastian said, noticing her hesitation. "I'm afraid there's no other way in or out. Not for us." Rose had a hundred questions she wanted to ask him, but there was something about his manner, coolly and unfailingly polite, that made her hesitant to speak. Perhaps it was the recollection of that brief, fleeting look when he'd first seen her, a look that could easily have been hatred or something like it. So she bit down on her questions and swallowed them back, made her face a meek and placid blank, and began slowly ascending the ladder, rung by hideous rung. These bones, at least, had been cleaned of any flesh, and Sebastian held the ladder steady for her from the bottom until she had reached the top, where a plump and freckled hand reached out through the window to help her in.

From the outside, the tower was no larger around than an elevator shaft. From the inside, it was immense, with great vaulted ceilings and wide archways leading in every direction. Every surface was black marble, polished and smooth and pleasantly cool against Rose's sore and bleeding feet. The room she entered now was so large she could barely see as far as the walls. In the far corner of the room, several women sat cross-legged around what appeared to be a pile of hair, patiently braiding the strands and chatting happily to one another in low soft voices.

It was a woman who had helped Rose through the window and into the tower—middle-aged, fat and motherly, with wisps of grey in her mousey brown hair and a pleasant homely face, one fat and hairy mole just beneath her eye. Only her lips and the tip of her tongue, black and blue, betrayed that she was dead. She spoke in breathy, rapid French, too fast for Rose to follow clearly, and impulsively opened her arms and stepped forward as if to embrace her, only restraining herself at the last moment, so that she rather hugged the air immediately surrounding Rose. Perhaps she was reluctant to get blood all over herself. She stepped back again, clasping her hands in front of her breast, still talking rapidly and incomprehensibly, and Rose had to interrupt, in her own awkward and limited French, apologizing and asking her to speak more slowly and simply, or in English if she could.

Apparently the woman couldn't speak English, but she did repeat herself more slowly and clearly, and Rose was able to make out some or most of it: that the woman's name was Jeanne-Marie; that Rose was just a poor child; that the woman was happy Rose was here, and that the queen would be happy, she was always so happy to see a young face, someone her own age; that Rose was a poor child again; and then she began speaking rapidly once more, as if she couldn't restrain herself, and Rose could follow no longer.

Sebastian appeared in the window now, coming lightly over the sill, and then he and Jeanne-Marie together pulled the ladder back in, carefully folding it up and placing it against the wall. The woman chattered happily away the entire time, with Sebastian occasionally saying, *Non*, or *Oui* in a polite and inattentive way.

Once the ladder had been taken care of, Sebastian asked Rose to come with him, and walked out through the central archway, past the women braiding—who smiled beatifically at Rose but did not speak—and down the corridor, still carrying his sack of apples. Rose followed, and Jeanne-Marie followed her with a mop made of a long branch and a bundle of rags tied to one end with a rope of hair, wiping up the bloody footprints that Rose left behind.

"We all serve the queen," Sebastian was saying, as he led her confidently through the twists and turns of the corridors to a thick oak door. "You'll get to serve her too, and know how sweet it feels. And one day, if you serve her well, you too shall be set free." It was a well-rehearsed speech, something he had no doubt repeated many, many times, to many different people.

Sebastian opened the door to a broad, round stairwell that went both down and somehow up, though they ought to have been at the very top and limit of the tower. He started down the stairs, and Rose still followed—still meek, still quiet, still careful—and Jeanne-Marie followed her still, mopping her path.

"Tell me, Rose," Sebastian asked, "how did you choose to die?" And then, after she had told him, he asked her if, before she died, she had been ill, whether she had suffered from any kind of contagious disease. "We have to be careful, you see, that the queen doesn't get sick, herself." They were still going down, flight after flight.

"But isn't she really dead, just like the rest of us?"

"She died before she was born, and in death she came to life." He said the phrase in a practised, mechanical way, as one who has repeated it many times, a kind of formal and religious incantation. Behind her, Rose could hear Jeanne-Marie repeat it, or something very like it, murmuring it in French beneath her breath, as one in church might repeat the preacher's words. A shudder went up between Rose's shoulder blades.

"She grows and becomes older," Sebastian continued. "She gets hurt and she heals. No one knows what would happen if she were to become sick, or mortally injured. No one knows what will happen when she grows old enough to die. No one knows if she *can* die again, but if or when she did, we'd all be lost, completely lost. Do you know how long you have been dead, Rose?"

"I don't know. Four, five months. Half a year, maybe?"

"That is all? And you have found the centre already? You are one of the lucky ones, then. Most of us wandered for years and years before we made it here. Years, decades, centuries. The queen will like you too," he said, and again she sensed a pulse of hostility beneath his outwardly courteous manner.

They had arrived finally at the bottom of the stairwell, and another wooden door, this one smaller, drab and stained. Sebastian knocked, and waited, and there was no response. "More and more pilgrims are arriving at the tower all the time," he said. "We used to go for days, weeks, without anyone coming to us; there was once a time when we would have to brave the city to spread the word and bring new pilgrims back. Now they wash up on our shore every day. Soon they will come in floods. The queen will never be able to free us all. Only a tiny fraction, the chosen few, shall be released."

"I saw her," Rose blurted out. "Sitting on the rocks, eating an apple. She spoke to me. She said I stink. Then she ran away when she heard your voice, she told me not to tell you." Sebastian's face as she spoke become coldly devoid of expression, but Jeanne-Marie at her back broke into an excited, joyous babble.

He opened the door, and waved her into a smallish, shabby room where the floor was made of compacted earth instead of marble, with a few scattered pale and stunted blades of grass struggling to grow. There was a hole, several feet wide, in the middle of the floor, and a distant sound like running water; there were stacks and piles of skulls and bones, braided hair and bloody rags and rotting apples heaped along the walls. Dropping the sack of apples to the ground, he said, "Jeanne-Marie will help you get clean." Then he left them there, closing the door firmly behind him.

Jeanne-Marie told Rose to remove her clothes, and she was glad to strip off her dress; it was drenched in blood, and felt hot and sticky and disgusting against her body. But when it came down to the tie, Bethany's tie, she hesitated. "Please," she said. "*S'il vous plait*. I'd like to keep this, it means something to me."

The woman clucked disapprovingly, and brusquely unknotted the tie herself. It's time to let go of such things, she said, or something like it. Let go of earthly things and start a new life. Then, more gently, she told Rose that at least they should take it to the laundry and have it cleaned. Perhaps it could be returned to her after, if it was so important.

Jeanne-Marie threw Rose's bloody clothes in a pile by the door. She took then a skull that was tied to a rope of hairs and lowered it into the hole. Rose heard a splash; the woman drew it carefully back up, and showed it to her: miraculously, it held a little water, real water, perfectly clear. Rose had never dreamed she might see real water again. Don't be tempted to drink it, the woman warned her, speaking slowly and clearly and pressing her hand on her stomach as she pantomimed the act of vomiting. She lifted the skull and dribbled the water over Rose's head, and then handed it to her, gesturing towards the well and inviting her to draw more.

As she did, the woman took another skull, and placed a crab-apple inside it. Then using a bone as a pestle, she began smashing and grinding the apple into a paste, talking merrily all the while, much of it enthusiastic effusions about the queen, *la reine douce et belle*, how sweet and beautiful, wondrous and gracious she was. Sometimes she would ask Rose questions about herself, but she generally didn't wait for an answer before babbling on again.

Rose dropped the skull in the well and drew it out, over and over again; she found that it was difficult to pull it up without most of the water leaking out through the eye sockets, and often came up with no more than a bare trickle. Meanwhile, she was longing to ask about her sister, whether Bethany was here in the tower too, or had been here. Longing to ask, but also afraid; afraid to learn that Bethany wasn't here, that she hadn't found the centre and was still out there somewhere, wandering, suffering, and lost; or perhaps worse, to learn that Bethany had come and was already gone, that she was one of the chosen few who had already been released.

Jeanne-Marie took the paste she'd made of the apple, seed and skin and all, scooped it out with her hand and slopped it into Rose's hair, rubbing it in vigorously, brusquely, as though Rose were a small and recalcitrant child being given a bath. It wasn't unpleasant. As Rose continued drawing more water from the well to wash it out, Jeanne-Marie began grinding more apples, this time to rub the paste all over the girl's body, scrubbing it against her skin in a rough maternal fashion, and Rose could have almost cried, it felt so good. Then Jeanne-Marie took a second skull and rope, and the two began drawing up water together. As together they bathed her, Rose summoned up her courage and asked about her sister.

Jeanne-Marie hardly seemed to be listening at first, and Rose wondered if her French was simply too rudimentary to make herself understood; but then the woman grew excited, understanding at last, and began saying "*Oui, oui, mais oui,*" and talking so fast again that Rose had to beg her to slow down and start over, her own heart pounding with something dangerously close to joy.

Bethany *was* here, and still here, it seemed. She had arrived some weeks ago, and had instantly become a favourite of the queen, who adored her. She hadn't been set free, not yet, but—and here Rose's tenth-grade French let her down, for she couldn't follow what Jeanne-Marie was saying, though the good woman patiently repeated and rephrased it several times. Bethany hadn't yet been set free, but she had been chosen to be, or was beginning to be, or was in the process of being set free. It was all very vague and confusing, and left Rose feeling uncertain and uneasy.

"Please," she begged, "*S'il vous plaît, je dois la voir*—I have to see her, before it's too late."

Jeanne-Marie reassured her, making a soothing clucking sound, rather as though Rose were an agitated chicken. She would see her sister soon enough, when it was time for *dévotion de matin.*

For them, of course, there was neither day nor night; there was no morning, afternoon or evening. But here in the tower they counted time according to the queen, and she was their sun who rose in the morning and set in the evening. Meaning, of course, that they called it "night" whenever the queen went to sleep, and "morning" when she got out of bed.

And every morning, after the queen had bathed if she felt like bathing and eaten breakfast if she was hungry, they would summon everyone together for the morning devotion, and the queen would speak to them, and meet and welcome any new pilgrims who might have arrived to join her service. And it was at morning devotion that the queen would choose who, if anyone, would be set free that day. If the spirit so moved her, she might even start the process of releasing the chosen one, right then and there.

After the devotion, Jeanne-Marie said, Rose would be introduced to the other servants. She would be assigned someone to help her learn the ways of the tower, and given a job. There were always many jobs to do, and that was a blessing, for it distracted from the pain. They all suffered, but to keep busy and useful and clean was the best remedy. And so, she said, even if you are never blessed to be chosen to become one with our queen, you will see that merely serving her is its own reward.

There were many jobs, from laundering and mending clothes, to braiding hair and polishing bones, sewing, weaving, making and repairing tools, sharpening the knives, mending the drums, taking care of the canoes. Those who could sing practised in the choir, for the queen liked to hear music around her, singing and drumming and dancing. There were the days to count and the calendar to keep. There was drawing water and gathering apples, watching the entranceway and tending to the ladder, helping new pilgrims as they arrived or preparing those chosen for release. And, of course, the cleaning—there was never any end of cleaning to do, Jeanne-Marie said, with a sigh that conveyed both weariness and pleasure. The floors and walls had to be washed constantly, there was always so much blood. Everybody bled. And then the rags would have to be constantly laundered to clean with them, and taken very good care of. Rose's dress would be cleaned and mended as best they could manage, used for clothing if they could salvage it, or cut into rags for cleaning or for bandages if they couldn't. Rose might be assigned to any of these jobs, according to her skills; or she might be chosen for the most rewarding job of all, waiting on the queen, keeping her company and satisfying her wishes. It would all be decided after the morning devotion.

It was, she told Rose, morning right now. In fact, it was already past time for the bell to ring and summon them all together, but the queen that morning had snuck out of bed and slipped out of the tower instead of bathing and breakfasting, and she couldn't be found. She did that sometimes. Usually she was only gone for an hour or two, but now and then she would disappear for a day or several days.

Poor child, said Jeanne-Marie, it must get so tedious for her here in the tower, so boring for a bright lively girl. For them, they had all lived their lives already, and endured years or even centuries of death beyond their lives. There was nothing any of *them* desired but to stay safely in the tower, serve the queen, and pray for release. But for Her Majesty, well, she was young and fresh and full of life. She wanted to see and experience new things, it was only natural. And then, of course, she was sixteen now, such a dangerous age, especially for a girl.

Sometimes the queen would disguise herself as a sufferer and go out into the city to look around. She didn't need the boat to come and go, though there was no one left who knew how she did it. They always begged her not to, it was far too dangerous, or at least, if she was absolutely determined to go—and of course no one could actually stop her—to take an escort of bodyguards with her. But there was no reasoning with a queen, of course, no more in death than there had been in life, and even less reasoning with a teenage girl. Here Jeanne-Marie apologized with a happy laugh, remembering that Rose was a teenage girl herself, but then, you see, *c'est différent, parce que vous êtes l'un de nous*—but the queen would do what the queen would do. At such times as she disappeared they could only wait in terror, trying not to imagine what would become of them all if she were never to return.

In the meantime, they did their best to keep her entertained here at the tower, so that she would be less likely to wander into the city in search of distraction. They did this, Rose gathered, by way of gossip and scandal, what the Frenchwoman called *petites comédies*. They would pretend to engage in romances and dramatic love triangles, politicking and intrigues, fights and falling-outs and making-ups between them; they would constantly backbite and gossip about one another to her, forming cliques and making accusations and counter-accusations, all to keep Her Majesty entertained and interested in what was going on among her servants in the tower, and to discourage her from going away for any length of time, lest she miss any exciting developments—rather as though they were all engaged in staging a live and perpetual soap opera for the queen's constant amusement.

It was great fun, Jeanne-Marie assured Rose, and they all enjoyed imagining new twists and turns to fill the next day, but Rose had to wonder if everyone was able to play these little comedies in such good humour and generous spirit as Jeanne-Marie. And she found herself marvelling at the woman a little, and loving her very much, and wondering how someone so good-hearted and optimistic and full of faith could ever, ever have even dreamed of killing herself in the first place. It hardly seemed possible. But then, perhaps Jeanne-Marie had been different in life; perhaps she had changed since coming here—she had been dead for over a century. Rose felt that she herself had changed since her death, and that was hardly half a year ago. Or perhaps there was something about the queen and being near the queen that had changed her.

Jeanne-Marie left Rose alone now, to take her bloody dress to the laundry and find her something clean to wear. Though she was still in pain, freezing cold and ferociously hungry, Rose felt cleaner and safer and more human, somehow, than she had since the night she had died. And as she was waiting for Jeanne-Marie to return, and trying in her mind to translate some of the dozens of questions she longed to ask, a bell began to toll.

She felt the sound in her body as much as she heard it with her ears. There was only a single bell, but it must have been massive, for the walls and floors vibrated with the sound, and the skulls and bones clattered in their little heaps. It rang again, and Jeanne-Marie came running back into the room, flushed with excitement. She had a man's white shirt in her hands, torn in the sleeve and missing two buttons, and she dressed Rose hurriedly, talking so quickly that Rose couldn't make out any words but *dévotion* and *rapide, rapide*. The shirt came down to her knees, the sleeves draped down past her hands, but Jeanne-Marie would not wait to roll them up, she fastened the remaining buttons with shaking fingers, grabbed the empty end of one sleeve, and hurried Rose up the stairs.

Still the bell continued to toll in a solemn and reverberant crescendo. There were many others on the stairs ahead of them and more pouring on at every landing, all hurrying up and up, their faces glowing with rapt anticipation. Those who were strong and whole helped those who were weak or lame, and everyone smiled joyously at one another: they were going to see the queen.

They came at last to the top floor, and a vast chamber in which a great domed ceiling rose forty or fifty feet high at the centre. Prodigious stained-glass windows circled the dome, and each window depicted—in kaleidoscopic patterns of pink and blue, black and yellow and green and red—dozens of faceless men, women and children, all hanging by their necks from barren trees. Rose wondered if this tower had always been here from the city's beginning, waiting to be discovered, or if it had only come to be when the queen arrived to find it.

At the very top and centre of the dome, a great iron bell was suspended from the beams, now slowly coming to a rest. It must, Rose guessed, have been the size of an ambulance. A rope—a real hempen rope, not one of hair—hung down almost to the floor, where the queen herself sat cross-legged on the edge of her bed, a meager and shabby mattress made of bundled rags. Another girl sat on one side of her and Sebastian stood near her on the other side, but Rose could catch only a fleeting and tantalizing glimpse of them from the back of the pressing crowd.

A hundred people at least, perhaps more, were thronged together in the chamber, forming a hushed and expectant ring around the bed. They were all pressed close together. None wanted to get disrespectfully close to the queen, leaving a space of fifteen or twenty feet between the congregation and the bed. The whole throng of people oscillated and rippled constantly, humming with barely suppressed energy. Hands rubbed shoulders and backs, bodies swayed, heads bobbed and rolled, lips moved in silent fervent prayers. All were bandaged, battered, bruised and dripping blood, all had stained and strained and weary faces that flickered with hope and devotion.

Rose tried to make her way through the crush and throng towards the centre, but no one would make room for her to pass, and Jeanne-Marie was putting a hand on her shoulder and trying to pull her back, whispering something about patience.

"All I want to know is," the queen was saying irritably, "*am* I the queen or am I not the queen?" She was addressing Sebastian, but spoke loudly enough to be heard throughout the room, conscious of her audience.

"Of course, Your Majesty," Sebastian replied, calmly and deferentially. "Of course you are the queen."

"Then why didn't you tell me before? If I'm such a queen, why don't you ever tell me these things?"

"I'm sorry, Your Majesty. I had no way of knowing."

"Well, what good are you then?" she said cheerfully. "Not much good at all, are you? I'd release you right now, la, just to get rid of you, but then everyone would walk around not knowing things, hoping I'd release them too. It's all terribly unfair, you know."

"Yes, Your Majesty."

Rose was standing on her toes and craning her neck, but she could see nothing save for the top of Sebastian's head. Unable to bear it any longer, knowing that her sister must be here somewhere, in this room, she yelled out, "Bethany! Bethany!"

An astonished and agitated murmur rippled through the crowd. Bodies turned and jostled to see who had spoken, and those closest to Rose were staring at her with outrage, unease and dismay, but Rose was unabashed, and she shouted again, yelling, "Bethany, are you here?"

"La," she could hear the queen saying brightly above the commotion. "Bethany, I think someone's looking for you."

Rose tried pushing her way forward again, and someone in the crowd pushed back. A rough hand shoved her on the small of her back and she slipped on the slick and bloodied marble, falling forward against the people in front of her, who angrily jabbed their elbows against her chest. "Bethany," she yelled, "it's me, Rose!"

"Oooh, that's the girl I was telling you about," said the queen, who was now standing atop her bed and trying to see over the crowd. "Why don't they let her through?"

"Let the girl through," Sebastian commanded, and the crowd fell silent again, and shuffled and squeezed even closer together to make a path for her, resentful but obedient.

Rose darted forward. Her heart was pounding so hard and so rapidly she saw white and black spots in front of her eyes, and then she was free of the crowd and there was her sister, sitting at the queen's feet.

As Bethany raised her face blindly, Rose saw that where her sister's eyes should have been there were only red rags stuffed into the empty sockets, and blood streamed down her cheeks like tears, and she said, "Rose?" in a voice that sounded more confused than anything. Her hair was chopped from her head, in some places shaved right down to the scalp; her beautiful honey-brown skin was ashen and tinged with green, there was a red and livid mark around her throat, and she was shuddering all through her thin long body.

Since the day of Bethany's funeral, Rose had often fantasized about seeing her again, being reunited. She'd played and replayed the moment over a thousand times in her mind, as vivid as life, but now that the moment had actually come there was no relief, no happy cry, no warm and safe embrace. Her chest hurt and she felt her face screwing up, ugly with hot tears, and her arms and her legs were weak and would not move. And instead of Bethany drawing her close, holding her and comforting her and saying she was sorry for leaving her alone, like Rose had always imagined, instead Bethany was angry and cold, yelling, "What are you doing here? Why did you come here?"

"I'm sorry," Rose tried to say, but her voice was little more than a cracked, constricted whisper.

"You're what? You're *what?*" said Bethany, livid now with rage, getting clumsily to her feet and moving a few awkward and uncertain steps forward, almost but not quite in Rose's direction. She held her chin up in the air and wove her head blindly back and forth, as if searching with her ears.

"I'm sorry," Rose said again, a little louder, more firmly this time. She felt exactly like she had once when she was ten, and Bethany had yelled at her for sneaking into her room and trying on her things. Tears and mucus were streaming into her mouth now and dripping off her chin, and the blood from Bethany's eye sockets was streaming into *her* mouth and dripping from *her* chin, and she took a few more steps in Rose's direction, the right direction this time, her left arm outstretched and groping at the air.

Rose's legs finally obeyed her, and she hurried over to her sister and touched her, saying, "I'm here, I'm here," expecting at last the hug she had so longed for. But once Bethany touched her, and felt where she was, instead of embracing Rose she flailed out with her right hand clenched in a hard fist, a furious and aimless blow that glanced wildly across the side of Rose's neck, and then both girls fell to the ground, and Rose was sobbing, frightened and heartbroken and engulfed with shame and self-hatred. Bethany was splayed backwards on the floor, berating her still, calling her a little fucking idiot, stupid fucking little dummy, and the low fierce words were pounding over Rose's head like heavy waves.

"You're not supposed to be here," Bethany screamed, crawling away from her, groping for the bed. "You idiot, you fucking little idiot, why did you want to fucking *die?*" And Rose was saying, "I'm sorry, I'm sorry, I'm sorry," desperately through her sobs, but she could scarcely breathe, let alone speak, she was crying so hard.

No one else in the room moved, nor made a sound. And then the queen did speak, and in a cheerful and brightly interested stage whisper said to Sebastian, "They seem a little upset."

"Yes, Your Majesty," said Sebastian quietly, inclining his head.

"It seems funny, Sebastian, but I really think they must have met before."

"Your Majesty, I believe they must be sisters. They look very much alike, I noticed it before."

"Well for goodness sake," the queen complained, narrowing her eyes. "Does everyone look like someone else all of a sudden? No one ever looked like anyone before she came, now everyone's looking like everyone. I suppose they do look a bit alike. I didn't notice it before. Of course when I saw her this morning she was all covered in blood. It's difficult to look like someone else when you're covered in blood, people should really keep that in mind. It isn't fair at all."

Rose by this time had stopped sobbing, but she remained on the floor, still curled up, fetal, hiding her face, ashamed.

"Do you really think they're sisters, though?" the queen chattered on happily. "That's very exciting. I always wished *I* had a sister, you know. Someone to share my lonely childhood with. I had a *very* lonely childhood, Sebastian," she said severely.

"Yes, Your Majesty."

"And I always longed for a sister."

"Yes, Your Majesty."

"And if I ever *did* have a sister, I'd certainly never punch her in the neck. Why should Bethany want to punch her sister in the neck, Sebastian? If you're so smart, why don't you tell me that? La, I don't believe they're really sisters at all. Bethany wouldn't punch her sister in the neck. She's never punched *me* in the neck. I know I'd remember that. I don't believe she's ever punched anybody in the neck, why would she start with her own sister? You might not know this, Sebastian, because you aren't a girl, but sisters love each other and brush each other's hair. They don't run around punching one another in the neck. Next time think before you go accusing people of having sisters. You're always making things up, Sebastian, I've spoken to you about it before, you know."

"I'm sorry, Your Majesty."

"There's no use in being sorry, you silly ass," she said cheerfully. "Just stop doing it, that's all."

Bethany by now had found the bed, and pulled herself onto it, huddled and angry. The queen crouched down beside her, and said, "That isn't really your sister now is it, Bethany?"

There was a long, uncomfortable silence, and then Bethany said, "Yes, Your Majesty," in a muffled, sullen voice. "She is."

"Really?" said the queen, delighted. "But that's so exciting!" She clapped her hands twice in front of her breast and skipped lightly down from the bed, turning a little pirouette on the floor and saying, "La, la, I knew it, I knew she was your sister! Oh, Bethany, my friend, you must be so, so happy to see her again, and I'm so happy *for* you. We'll have a feast! You know I was going to release you today, but now that your sister's come to see you, of course you won't want to go."

"No," said Bethany, "no, please…"

"Oh, don't worry about me, silly," said the queen affectionately. "I'll release someone else instead, that's all. It will be a great celebration."

She chose Bethany's replacement seemingly at random, out of the feverish, pained and desperate faces in the crowd. The woman she chose began to tremble and sweat as she stepped forward, and the people behind her murmured excitedly, some faces suffused with empathetic pleasure, some twisted, flushed and ugly with envy or disappointment. Bethany, on the bed, had covered her face and was crying. But to all this, all the raw and pained emotion around her, the queen remained cheerfully oblivious, smiling pleasant and benign as she said to the woman, "Would you like that? Are you ready to go?"

The woman couldn't speak, but she nodded her head vigorously, shaking so hard as the queen spoke to her, she seemed as though she were about to fall down in a seizure.

"Oh, good. La, let's start now, I'm absolutely starving, all this talk of sisters and people looking like other people and punching each other in the neck, I feel like I haven't eaten in weeks." She turned to Sebastian then and said, "I'll have her eyes right away,

Sebastian, just something to tide me over for now. They're always the loveliest bit anyway, la. And then we'll have a big feast this evening. It'll be such a celebration! There will have to be songs, Sebastian, I want to hear lots of singing—something about sisters. Has anyone ever written a song about sisters, do you think?"

"I'm sure we can think of some, Your Majesty," he said, with a low cold bow, and his face was cold and pale and restrained with a courteous and a careful hate.

"Well, you might sound a little more enthusiastic, Sebastian," the queen complained. "Aren't you happy for my sweet Bethany?"

As the preparations were being made, the people gathered around the woman, congratulating her, shaking her hand, hugging and kissing her, much as you would for a bride on the day of her wedding, saying in a dozen different languages, "We'll miss you," and "I'm so happy for you," and, "Be at peace." That was the most often repeated phrase, for those too full of envy, pain or weariness to feel sincerely happy for someone else, they would smile a false disheartened smile and say, "Be at peace." Through all this the woman still could barely speak, but she nodded and smiled and hugged her friends, sometimes crying, sometimes laughing at herself for crying, and all in all, thought Rose, looking as much terrified as she did excited.

At last the ceremony was ready to begin. The woman's clothes were taken from her body, folded and carried away. At first she made an effort to cover her chest, where a mastectomy in life had left one breast a small uneven bump with a thick and jagged ugly scar across the middle, but firm and loving hands pushed her to her knees and pulled her arms away. Her hair was cut from her head with an old steak knife, sawing it off as close to her scalp as possible, and her face was carefully scrubbed clean with a wet rag. Once she was clean, the queen stepped up to her, gave her a gentle and ceremonial kiss on the centre of her forehead, and then stepped back away.

The woman let out a gasp and a long, keening wail, arching and twisting her torso, scuffling her knees frantically on the marble floor, straining against the men who held her arms, straight out and pinned back against their bodies. The man who had cut off her hair put his hand on either side of her head and held it steadily, squeezing forcefully. Most of the people in the crowd had closed their eyes and lowered their heads, repeating whispered fervent prayers. It was Sebastian who stepped up to the woman now, holding a small paring knife, and he said, "Be at peace," in a solemn voice. The gathered crowd echoed back the words: "Be at peace." Then Sebastian pried the woman's right eyelid open with his finger and thumb, inserted the point of the knife carefully in the corner of her eye, right at the tear duct, and pushed. The woman screamed so loud it made the great iron bell above them reverberate and hum.

# 17

THE NEXT COUPLE WEEKS WERE PRETTY CRAZY. EVERYTHING was so busy and we barely got any sleep with the baby crying on and off all night, and Addy always up and about at weird hours, and when I did sleep I had all kinds of nasty dreams. I just walked around in a kind of haze, with a head full of spiderwebs. And then the house was so crowded with people all the time, I thought I was going to go nuts.

It was just too cold to go out, Davey was home, Tante Martine was there pretty much all day, every day, you had Mom and the baby and Addy staying with us on top of it. It was too much. And then other people were constantly dropping by as well—Conrad and his parents and his Nana, the neighbours, Mom and Davey's co-workers from the restaurant, all of their friends. Everybody wanted to meet the baby, and they all brought presents too, and bottles of wine, and Christmas baking. We had little platters of shortbread cookies and rum balls and gingerbread men and boxes of chocolate piling up on every countertop and table, and heaps of board books and little soft shoes and hideous pink frilly baby clothes and stupid plastic toys still in their packages. And everybody who dropped by, Davey would make them come in and sit down and have a drink, or two, or three, until Mom completely freaked out and said that if one more person came into her house, she was going to beat them to death with a baby rattle.

Of course everybody loved Madeline, she was so small and sweet and scared and helpless, with her little fists in their mittens and her little eyes that could hardly open, crying all the time, how could you not love her? Mom made a big deal out of everyone calling her by her full name, not Maddy for short, and it had to be Made*line*, like rhyming with nine or shine, she got really picky about how people pronounced it.

Her eyes were blue, just like Mom and Jack's. Mom told me that newborn babies always have blue eyes and I did too, that they usually change after a year or two. "I don't know," I said. "Casey told me one time that Addy's eyes were green right from the moment she was born, and two different shades of green already, too."

"Honey, Casey says a lot of things that aren't true," Mom said wearily. And then she said, "Oh, sorry, Addy."

"Hey, no skin off my butt," said Addy cheerfully. She was down on her hands and knees on the kitchen floor, holding her nose a bare centimetre from the baby's and making frowny monster faces at her. "Boo," she whispered solemnly. "Boo."

Madeline seemed to like it, too, though Mom insisted she was only passing gas. She was sitting in her car seat, with her fuzzy pink sleeper, and those little white socks over her fists so she wouldn't scratch herself. And that baby loved Addy, oh my God. If anyone else but Mom tried to pick her up or hold her, even Davey, she'd scream like she was being tortured to confess. But Addy would pick her up and put her little nose in the hollow of her neck, and you could just see her whole body unclench, she'd murmur a bit and fall straight to sleep. And it was funny, too, because you know Tante Martìne had this weird thing about Addy. Davey said she had some crazy superstition about people with two different coloured eyes, like they were demon spawn or something, which of course pleased Addy immensely. Anyway, she kept telling Davey to tell Mom to keep "that child" away from the baby, so it was funny that Madeline loved Addy so much but she'd scream and scream and scream if Tante Martìne came anywhere near her.

Me, I only tried holding her twice. The first time I nearly dropped her, she wriggled and writhed and cried so hard. The second time she just spat up all down my shirt the moment I picked her up. But I did help change her diaper a lot. That was Addy's idea, she said that it's just like the way a cat always ends up loving whoever changes its litter box all the time. So whenever Madeline needed a diaper change, which felt like pretty much all the time, Addy and I would offer to do it, Addy would play with her and talk to her and keep her entertained at the top while I'd do the diaper and wipe her up at the bottom. I got to be pretty expert at it.

On Christmas Eve I woke up a couple hours after I'd gone to sleep. I remember thinking how still and peaceful and quiet the house seemed, for really the first time in days. Maybe that's what woke me up. Outside it was snowing lightly, Addy above me was purring gently in her sleep, and I wanted a glass of water. My mouth was all dry.

When I came around the hallway, I saw that Mom and Davey were awake, sitting in the living room in the dark. Only the lights of the Christmas tree were on, softly washing them in red and green and blue. They were both in their bathrobes; Mom was feeding the baby at her breast, and Davey was sitting close beside them, one hand holding Mom's hand, the other gently playing with her hair. They never did notice me, and I stood there a minute or so, watching them from the hall. They looked exhausted, but absolutely happy, and utterly in love. Davey leaned in and whispered something in Mom's ear, then brushed her cheek with his lips. Mom smiled, laughed silently. Madeline squirmed contentedly in her arms and sucked away greedily, occasionally making a kind of squeaking noise like a little brown mouse.

I wondered if Mom and my father had looked happy like that after Jack was just born. Of course when I was a newborn baby, my father was already gone. And I remember thinking that it was too bad for Davey that Jack and I were even around at all. I knew he loved us and even liked us, but we weren't really his, not the way Madeline was and always would be.

I tiptoed back to my room. I didn't want them to notice me, I didn't want to spoil their moment. It was probably the first bit of peace they'd had since the baby came.

I lay in bed, awake, a long time that night. I was so tired I wanted to scream but I couldn't get back to sleep, I couldn't shut my brain off. And I couldn't turn on the light and read, I couldn't go watch TV or get something to eat, sit in the kitchen, I couldn't do anything without disturbing someone. All I could do was lie there in the dark, like I was trapped there in my bed, like there was no other place or space for me in my own house any more.

It was funny, too, cause it was Christmas Eve. You know, how many times had I lain awake like this on Christmas Eve, when I was just a little kid, unable to sleep but not wanting to move? Maybe Addy even sleeping in the bunk above me. But of course this was completely different. Back then I couldn't sleep because I was too excited, thinking about what presents I'd find beneath the tree, thinking about the presents I'd bought for other people and whether they'd really love them, wondering if I'd hear Santa when he came, afraid that he'd know I was still awake and wouldn't come at all, thinking about what was the earliest possible time I could get up and say it was morning now and not still night. You know how you get when you're so excited about something that it almost feels the same as being terrified, you almost feel sick even? And I wondered if maybe I would never get to feel that excited about anything again, maybe only little kids ever really feel that way. And I thought about how Madeline had all that still ahead of her, but for me it was over, and maybe for me a lot of things were over. And I felt angry at Madeline a little, though I knew it was stupid. But I felt it all the same, I couldn't help it, I was angry that she'd been born early like this and stole my time with Addy. This might be the last Christmas Addy and I would ever spend together, maybe the last time she'd ever come and stay with us, I'd been looking forward to it for so long and thinking about all the things we'd do together, but now Madeline had come and she was the centre of everything.

I thought about so many things, I couldn't stop it. And I thought, at last, about Rose. The wind had picked up outside the house and the snow was coming down hard now, rattling the window, and I thought about the phone call from Rose's mother. I had practically forgotten about until just then, everything had been so overwhelming. And I felt ashamed that I hadn't done anything about it, hadn't done anything to help. But what could I have done anyway? I thought about Tim and Janine and what kind of Christmas Eve they must be having, not knowing maybe where their daughter was, maybe not even knowing if she was dead or alive, and how probably they were drunk.

Maybe it was okay after all, maybe Rose had come home or called and everything was all right, but somehow I felt certain that it wasn't, and she never would. And I hated myself for not having been a better friend, for having lost touch with Rose and having not tried harder; and then I sort of hated myself for feeling that way, too, because of course it wasn't really about me, I shouldn't feel like I was so important. And I thought how there are two kinds of people in the world, the kind who leave and the kind who get left behind. Addy is the kind who leaves, of course, just like her grandma was, just like my father was, just like Bethany was. But I'd always thought that Rose was one of the left behind kind, like me, only I guess she was braver than I was, and she was a leaver too.

At some point I stopped thinking and I started dreaming, I dreamt that I slipped out of bed and snuck out of the house, right then and there, and went searching for Rose, winding up and down the dark streets, through the blinding snow, calling out her name. Then the dream shifted, it wasn't snowing any more and I was walking through Beaconsfield Park, and there were dozens of bodies dangling from the trees, hundreds even—a body hanging by the neck from every branch, swaying in the wind. And I was walking beneath them, looking up and examining every face, but I don't think I was looking for Rose any more. I don't remember. Maybe I was looking for me. And then it was morning and I was awake, the house was bright with sunlight and I could smell breakfast cooking in the kitchen, and I lay in bed and listened to the sound of Jack and Addy and Mom and Davey all chatting and laughing in the kitchen.

# 18

BETHANY TOLD ROSE THAT AFTER THEY CUT OUT HER EYES, SHE could still see through them, she could see everything. She told Rose about it more than once. She kept returning to it, helplessly, reliving it over and over.

When they had placed her eyes on the dish, of course they had made no effort to have them pointing in the same direction, and she could see virtually the whole chamber, in a great fish-eye round. She had even been able to see herself, naked and contorted and gushing blood, arms and head restrained as they stuffed the rags in her eye sockets; screaming, shrieking, thrashing and twisting her body, kicking her legs wildly as she was half-dragged, half-carried from the chamber.

The pain was excruciating, searing, unbearable, but the seeing was worse. She couldn't move her eyes, she couldn't close them or focus them, all she could do was watch helplessly, her field of vision floating across the room as the dish was carried to the queen, blurry bodies and ghostly faces flitting around the periphery, and then the queen's cheerful face looming above her, freckled and enormous. She could *feel* her eyes too. She could feel it when the queen picked one up between her fingernails, feel the warmth and wetness when she put it in her mouth, feel the pain when she bit down. That felt like a bomb going off inside her skull, she said, but once the queen had chewed and swallowed it down, that pain stopped, and so did the seeing, and the relief was overwhelming. Blindness was better, infinitely better.

She and Rose were alone in the queen's chamber now, on the bed, beneath the bell. The queen herself had gone. Having tried and failed to get them to tell her about what it was like to have a sister and how wonderful it must be, she had quickly grown bored and petulant, announced loudly that she had to go take a piss, and then simply disappeared.

One of the servants had remained with them in the chamber for several minutes after the queen had left, diligently sopping the blood up from the floor, until they heard five hollow knocks in a little rhythmic pattern reverberate up the walls.

"Another new pilgrim," the woman said wearily, shaking her head as she got to her feet. "I'd better go and see if I can help." And she gathered up the bloody rags, gave Rose a sad and sympathetic smile, and headed for the stairs.

Rose held her sister tight, and rocked her in her arms, and caressed her wounded scalp and the sparse tufts of remaining hair. It was hard for her to believe that this was really Bethany, this broken shell. She tried to calm her down, comfort her, but Bethany could not be comforted. Sometimes she lay limply against her sister, crying like an infant; sometimes she pushed her away, lashing out, swinging her fists in rage. It wasn't fair, she kept saying, over and over again. It was supposed to be her turn now; her time to be released and set at peace. It would be her right now if Rose hadn't shown up and ruined it.

"How do you know?" said Rose. "How do you know you'd be at peace? Maybe it isn't peace at all," she said, "maybe you go to something even worse, you just don't know." But Bethany wouldn't listen, told her to shut up, stop saying that, you don't understand, and she dug her nails into Rose's arms so hard she drew blood but Rose wouldn't let her go.

Bethany refused to go to the feast. She stayed behind, alone, crying in the queen's great chamber. Rose wanted to stay behind too, stay with her sister, she never wanted to leave her again, but Bethany had screamed at her to go away, so that it almost broke her heart, and Sebastian had placed his hand gently on her shoulder and led her away.

"I know it must be hard for you," he said, "but it's best to leave her be. I've seen this many times before. We can hardly imagine the pain she must be suffering. No one can do anything for her now, I'm afraid, except the queen."

All day long, the tower and the island had buzzed with activity, in preparation. The chosen woman had first been dragged down to the basement and thoroughly and carefully bathed; she was then taken back up to the high window and thrown from the tower, falling the hundred feet to burst against the ground below. They said it made her easier to butcher that way, for she couldn't struggle so much with her bones all shattered, and with any luck her skull would be split, making it easier to get at the brains. They were very careful to get every last fragment and morsel of brain out, to be eaten and digested; they made sure that not the smallest particle would be left behind, to possibly hold a thought or memory or emotion in its cells.

The woman was butchered down on the banks, along the rocks where Rose had passed with Sebastian and seen the boats. Her brains and heart and tongue and flesh were chopped and sliced into bite-sized pieces, the brains and heart placed carefully aside in two polished skulls to be eaten first, that afternoon. Some of the fat they smeared over slices of apple, to make a kind of dessert; the rest of the meat was wrapped in leaves from the apple trees and packed in woven baskets, to be eaten over the next few days.

Some of her bones would be saved and scraped and polished. But they already had so many, a whole room full of skulls and bones, Sebastian told her, that there seemed little point in saving more; most of them would be flung into the river, along with her entrails, bladder, spine, and other inedible bits.

It was Sebastian who led Rose the way to the high place, having come to fetch the queen; but the queen was already gone. "She said she had to go to the bathroom," Rose told him, "but that was, I don't know, two or three hours ago, maybe more? She just sort of disappeared, and didn't come back."

But Sebastian didn't seem concerned. "Her majesty will be there," he said confidently. "She'll come when she hears the drums, if she isn't there already." The feast took place outdoors, on a high and rocky place that hung over the river. He led Rose out of the tower and along a path that snaked up the hill, often pausing to wait politely as she clambered awkwardly and stiffly over the moss-covered rocks and fallen branches, but never offering a hand to help her.

Rose asked him if anyone had ever come to the island and then left again, ever decided they didn't want to be set free after all. "Some have," he said. "Many are afraid, disturbed, at first. But the longer they stay with the queen, the more they come to love her, and crave the glory and the peace of becoming one with her."

Everyone, of course, was free to leave. They would even be taken by one of the boats and helped back safely to the city, should they so choose. "Some have gone," he said, "but sooner or later everyone returns. They always find their way back eventually, and beg her Majesty to set them free."

Rose could hear the drums now, up in the distance; more people had joined them on the path, ahead of and behind them, travelling in groups of three or four, some solemn, some excited, some laughing.

"Is it always like this?" Rose asked, "A big party like this?" She couldn't quite keep the disgust, the outrage, entirely out of her voice or her face.

"We always celebrate when someone is released and set at peace," he replied severely. "We consider it to be an occasion worth celebrating. And we feel, too, that it is a way of thanking Her Majesty for what she must do for us, to show her how happy and how grateful we can be."

Among the people walking near them, Rose caught a glimpse of a familiar face: one of the men from the bridge, the one called Aaron. She recognized him with a shock, walking beside Jeanne-Marie, his eyes downcast, listening politely to her effusions, his doughy face pink and freshly washed. He must have been the one who had arrived earlier in the day, washed up on the island. Rose felt a surge of anger as she remembered him pushing past her on the bridge, remembered him stepping on Emmanuel's hand, remembered Emmanuel falling helplessly into the river. It was the first time she had really thought of her friend since she had arrived on the island. She wished that he were here with her now, to help her and to listen to her. She thought with horror that he must still be out there, in the river, unable to swim, unable to do anything but drown forever. I'll find him, she thought. I'll take one of those boats and go up and down the river as long as I have to, I won't just leave him out there, I won't.

They came at last to the top of the hill, where the ground was a shelf of stone and moss and brittle green-grey lichen. It was strange to look past the cliff and across to the city, at the roofs and backs of the crowded derelict houses in an endless line, like a different and distant world; and no sounds carried from there to the island, even on this high cliff there was no breath of wind.

The queen was there already, perched on a smooth high rock, one leg dangling down, and when she spotted Rose and Sebastian emerging from the path, she hopped lightly down and hurried over. "Where's Bethany?" she asked, raising herself on her tiptoes to look past their shoulders.

"I'm sorry, your majesty, but she refuses to come," Sebastian said. "You must remember she's in tremendous pain."

The queen made a face, scrunching up her nose and sticking out her tongue. "Oh, pain, pain, tremendous pain," she complained. "Everyone's always in tremendous pain, it's really very tedious. Now what's the point of celebrating Bethany getting a sister if Bethany isn't even going to be here to celebrate? La! I'm beginning to think," she said to Rose, "that she isn't very happy to see you after all. I expect you weren't a very good sister. She probably killed herself just to get away from you," she added cheerfully, "and now you've hunted her down just to bother her. Well, if Bethany won't come, maybe we ought to just cancel the feast completely, all this talk of pain has spoiled my appetite anyway."

"You know you can't do that, Your Majesty. We've already prepared Antonia for the feast, to not release her now would be unimaginably cruel."

"I know, I know, don't tell me, she's in tremendous pain. Well, I'll do it, Sebastian, because if I don't you'll all walk around moaning and making sad-eyes at me and all I'll hear is 'poor Antonia' this and 'poor Antonia' that, but I won't enjoy it, Sebastian. I won't enjoy it at all. In fact, tell them to put the drums away, I don't even want to hear any music, that's how disappointed I am, and I hope you all feel horrible."

Sebastian bowed, and went to speak to the drummers. "It really is too bad," the queen said to Rose. "Tell me, la, do you think he's terribly handsome?"

Rose, startled, said, "Sebastian? No, I don't, I don't at all."

"There you are, neither do I, but Jeanne-Marie is always telling me half the ladies here are falling in love with him. Have you met Miko? She's the one over there, with the black hair and that thing on her cheek, standing by the crooked pine. They say she's terribly jealous, but I just can't imagine why. Were you ever in love? I mean, when you were alive?"

"I don't know," said Rose. "A little bit, maybe."

"And were you terribly jealous? Is that why you killed yourself?"

"No," said Rose. "It wasn't. Why did you?"

"Oh, I don't remember," she said airily. "They always say I did it on purpose just so I could come here and save them, but that seems awfully silly. I expect I was upset, or bored, or something. I'm sure I must have had an excellent reason. La, I'd like to be in love, though. There was a boy who came here once I thought was cute, his name was Carlos and he had the bushiest eyebrows you've ever seen, but it's hard to really fall in love with someone who's constantly complaining about being in pain and begging you to eat his brains. People should really think about that before they decide to be in pain all the time, it's terribly unattractive."

"And did you... do this to him?"

"Oh, yes. He was really quite delicious, I was terribly sad about the whole thing. Did you hear that, Sebastian?" she said brightly as he rejoined them. "Rose thinks you're very ugly, too, so you shouldn't be so full of yourself. Well, are we going to begin?"

The drums had fallen silent and the people gathered along the cliff were looking towards their queen now with strained and troubled faces, but she smiled her brightest and most beguiling smile, waved her hand, and said loudly, "I'm absolutely famished. Bring me the food right away—and sing something, too, I want to hear some love songs, something nice and sad, la. Come," she said, slipping her warm soft hand over Rose's and pulling her with her towards the rock. "Tell me all about this girl you know who looks so much like me. What did you say her name was again?"

The drums were made of skin stretched over wooden frames, and the drummers beat them with their palms, and bones, and sticks, filling the air with a weird persistent rhythm. They showed no pleasure in drumming. Despite their efforts, the singers showed no pleasure in singing, the dancers no joy in dancing. All forced themselves to smile, but their faces were strung out with pain, grey and sagging and exhausted. Some pounded their drums or flung and spun their bandaged, crippled bodies around with a kind of violent ecstasy, as though trying to lose themselves in the movement and the rhythm, but most of them jerked dutifully in time like broken-down marionettes, exhausted, empty, past the limits of endurance, desperately trying to appear as if they were enjoying themselves. And the queen watched them happily, contentedly, as she daintily ate the brains of that butchered woman with her bare fingers, and tore at the long thin strips of the woman's sliced heart with her sharp small teeth.

"Brains are okay," she told Rose, "but most people's hearts are so tough, you wouldn't believe. This one isn't bad, but I've had some that were like an old shoe, you just can't imagine, and I just have to choke it down anyway or Sebastian will never stop nagging me. La, if I had my way I'd eat nothing but eyes and apples all the time, but I suppose that wouldn't really be fair. And anyway, who wants to be surrounded by hundreds of blind people, all bleeding and screaming and feeling sorry for themselves? It's depressing enough around here as it is."

She sat perched on her rock as she ate, dangling one dainty foot. Rose stood at her side, right near the edge of the cliff, where a spindly pine grew crookedly out over the drop, its roots clinging tenaciously to the stone and hard dry earth. Rose peered over the edge, down to where the wine red blood sprayed and foamed against the jagged black rocks. She had a brief intense vision of grabbing the queen and throwing her over the edge, to break her body on the rocks and drown in the blood below, and she shuddered.

"La," the queen said, her eyes sparkling as the singers and drummers began a lively song. Her lips were stained a luscious vibrant red. A bit of brain clung to the corner of her mouth. "Do you like to dance? I love this one, come dance with me." And she hopped lightly down from the stone, placing her baskets of food on the ground, and skipped to the middle of the clearing, where she started turning giddy pirouettes with her arms above her head, graceful and lithe. Her shadow floated over the moss and stone, her bare feet glided and stamped, her fiery long hair bounced and shimmered and swirled sinuously around her body. She tossed her head and sang off-key, she glowed with spontaneous and innocent delight, and laughingly she took one of the men by the hand and pulled him towards her.

# 19

WE ATE CHRISTMAS DINNER ON BOXING DAY, BECAUSE NO ONE had remembered to thaw out the turkey in time, so we decided to wait and do the turkey and stuffing and sweet potatoes and everything the next day. On Christmas Day itself we just ate Chinese take-out, because nothing else was open, and there wasn't really anything else in the house besides milk and cookies and chocolates and booze.

We ate dinner in the middle of the afternoon, while the baby was taking her nap, and we didn't even sit down properly at the table, we just ate in the living room with our plates on our laps. Mom made Addy phone her mother in Montreal to wish her a merry Christmas, but all she got was the answering machine. Then we went out around the circle and read out our fortune cookies, Jack's was something lame about collecting an old debt in the coming year, and mine was kind of dumb, it said, "You will get lost, and find what you were looking for." But Addy had an awesome one, hers said, "Never wear your best shirt to clean the bathroom." Addy always got the best fortune cookie fortunes.

Of course, we opened presents and stuff in the morning. Davey gave Mom a package of fuzzy wool socks, which surprised me cause usually Davey gives really thoughtful gifts. Mom didn't give Davey anything at all, cause she said she gave him a damn baby and what more did he want, but that didn't surprise me at all. And Addy gave me two bottles of nail polish, one black and the other one a dark burgundy. She made me let her paint my toes right then, that very morning. I chose the black. She wanted to do my fingernails too, but I drew the line at that, at least my toes nobody would see.

On New Year's Eve we spent the night at Conrad's—me and Jack and Addy. Davey arranged it, so that he and Mom could have the house to themselves for one night. Well, him and Mom and the baby.

It wasn't a party or anything, but it was fun. Just the four of us, and Conrad's parents and Nana, of course. His older brothers were out most of the night, and we had pizza and watched a couple movies and ate some popcorn. When it was getting close to midnight, Boris came down to the basement and told us to come all get our stuff on, he was going to set off fireworks in the back yard.

There was a light dusting of fresh snow over everything, so pretty the way it sparkled under the streetlights; the moon three-quarters full shimmered in the sky, and I counted seventeen stars. It was cold, but still. You could hear thumping music and drunken happy angry voices drifting up and down the street. Boris was as excited as a boy with a new toy, bustling about with his big cardboard box full of fireworks. He'd moved the car around to the front street so that he could set them off in the driveway. He gave us all sparklers, too, that we clutched in our mittens, but we weren't allowed to light them until midnight struck. A distant siren trailed by.

Addy volunteered to be Boris's assistant, and stood out on the driveway with him. The rest of us hung back on the deck. When it was almost midnight, someone very drunk a couple houses over yelled out the seconds counting down from his front stoop, ten-nine-eight, and when he got to zero, a staggered cheer went up and down the street, echoing loudly through the night, and there were popping sounds like guns going off, and half a dozen dogs or more barking and howling in agitated response. We cheered too. Addy and Boris lit the first firework, and it popped into the air and fizzled blankly out. They lit the second one, arguing animatedly, and it did the same, but the third one went off properly, a burst of cold white starlight in the black night sky. We cheered again, waved our sparklers in the air, spelling out swear words with the tracers of light. Another one went off—green, and then red—and then a really good one that spun in a pinwheel of blue sparks and left a spatter of black embers across the roof of the neighbour's garage. There were hoots and applause all up the street for that one, and the sound of breaking glass, and more sirens in the distance.

Conrad's mom said that was enough for her, and she was going inside to make hot chocolate for everybody. Jack went in too, he said it was just too damn cold and his lip was beginning to hurt. The next one that Boris and Addy set off was another dud, and they started arguing again. I was cold too, my nose was all froze and my cheeks were stinging, but I didn't want to go in yet. I felt as happy as I had felt in I don't know how long. I guess at least since that first night Addy had arrived. It was one of those moments you get when life just seems all right, all good, everything about it, and I didn't want that moment to end just yet. Conrad asked me if I was making any New Year's resolutions.

"Maybe," I said. "Isn't it bad luck to say them out loud, though? Like a birthday wish, if you tell people it won't come true?"

"I don't think so. You guys think everything is bad luck," he complained, looking over at Addy. He started breathing into his cupped hands to warm his face, and kind of stepping up and down in place. Another firework trailed up and burst in blue above our heads.

"Do you want to go inside?" I asked him.

"Not yet," he said. "Do you?"

"No, me neither. I like it out here."

"You know, I kind of miss walking to school with you every morning," he said awkwardly. "Seems like I don't see you that much any more."

"Yeah, me too, I guess." I was a little surprised, I thought we still saw one another around a lot, he and Jack were always hanging out together. But it was a nice thing to say, I figured he was just trying to be nice.

"So," he said again, insistently, "what's your New Year's resolution?"

I laughed. "Okay," I lied, "my New Year's resolution is to stop thinking that everything's bad luck so much. How's that?"

"That's okay," he said. "Not bad."
"What's yours, then? You have to have one if I do."
"Sure," he said. I think he was blushing, but it was hard to tell because he was already red from the cold. He looked over at his father and Addy, who were squatting down over the box of fireworks, arguing away, completely absorbed; and then, with a kind of startling suddenness and all in a rush, like someone who's screwed his courage up so much it almost resembles a panic attack, he darted in at me and kissed me on the mouth, bumping my face clumsily with his nose. He stepped back and glanced quickly over at his dad and Addy to make sure they hadn't seen.

I was stunned... it was stupid. I think I just stood there with my mouth hanging slack, staring at him. I wanted to say or do something but I couldn't think of *anything*. I don't know how long I just stood there motionless, with my brain just totally refusing to function, but it must have felt like a really long time to Conrad because he finally just mumbled something like, "I'd better go inside," and then said, "Sorry," as he rushed into the house. I think I said, "Wait," but not till he'd already closed the door behind him. There was a big pop and a holler of pain from the driveway, the last firework had gone off prematurely and Boris had got a bunch of blue sparks on the hood of his parka and all in his hair.

When I told Addy that Conrad had kissed me, what he'd said and everything, she said it was obviously because of the nail polish. "It makes you irresistible," she said.

"Don't be an idiot," I said back. "He didn't even see my toes."

"That just makes it even more powerful. It's like this secret mysterious aura, he doesn't know *why* you're suddenly irresistible but there's just something about you..."

"I'm being serious," I said. "Why would he want to kiss me like that?"

She gave me a strange look, with her eyes quite wide and extremely green. "Why not?" she said, in a reasonable-person sort of voice. "I don't know why you're so surprised, why wouldn't he want to kiss you?" I didn't say anything; it didn't seem that way to me, and anyway, I wasn't fishing for compliments, I was trying to figure out what I should do.

"You goof," she said affectionately. "You're cute and you're awesome and you have sexy black toes, guys are gonna want to kiss you, get used to it. Was it a good kiss at least?"

"It was cold," I said. "And quick. But it was nice, I think. What should I say to him? I can't believe I didn't say anything, I have to tell him something. Do you think he really meant it, or do you think it was maybe just an impulse sort of thing? Like the fireworks and stuff, maybe he just got sort of caught up in the moment, more than, you know?"

"Oh for goodness sake," she said, clearly losing interest. "What do you *want* to tell him?"

But that was the problem. I had absolutely no idea. You know I liked Conrad a lot, I liked hanging out with him and I guess I thought he was cute. I mean, I didn't think he *wasn't* cute or anything, I'd just honestly never thought about him that way at all. I wondered, too, how Jack would react, his best friend trying to make out with his little sister. You never knew with Jack.

Before we went home that day, I managed to get Conrad alone for a few minutes. He'd been avoiding that, and not making eye contact with me and stuff, but Addy helped engineer it.

When I had him trapped alone in the kitchen, I said, "Listen. Would you like to maybe ... I thought maybe we could go to a movie or something one night, just you and me. Your treat."

"Really?" he said.

"Yeah, really. You know, after Addy goes home and things settle down a little bit, it's pretty crazy right now, but you could give me a call after she's gone and we could just, you know, go out somewhere, whatever. If you want to."

"Yeah, I want to," he said. "I'd like that."

"And then, you know..." I'm sure I must have been blushing too, it felt so hot and awkward and dumb, but I said, "If you kissed me again at the end of the night, then I wouldn't be so surprised, and

I guess, you know, we'll see? I mean, only if you want to kiss me again. We could try. And see."

Conrad looked every bit as uncomfortable as I felt. It was actually kind of adorable, but he looked happy too, and he told me he'd really like that, and then he said, "Thanks, thank you."

"Don't thank me," I said. "I'm not doing you a favour." And that made him look confused and slightly frightened, so I gave him a kiss on the cheek, quickly said, "That didn't count," and then hurried out of the kitchen.

When we got home that afternoon, it was just a little after lunchtime. Davey was so drunk already he was making a batch of roti and Mom was all pouting and blushing and broody, but in a secretly happy sort of way, and Davey told us they'd got engaged, and made us each drink a glass of champagne. Mom had a ring on her finger and everything. He'd popped the question at midnight, when, as Mom said, she was delirious with exhaustion and her defenses were all down, as if he'd taken some kind of unfair advantage of a poor helpless innocent. Of course we were all thrilled, or at least Addy and I were, and we danced around the kitchen singing, "We're going to be bridesmaids, we're going to be bridesmaids," until Mom told us to shut the hell up and went to her room.

The day Addy flew back to Montreal, that was her and Jack's sixteenth birthday, January fifth. I always felt bad for them that they had their birthday right after the holidays like that, when everyone's all celebrated out, and the last thing anyone wants is another party, and they've already spent too much money on Christmas gifts and they don't want to spend any more on you. It's basically the shaft. We had cake before we went to the airport, and sang happy birthday to them both, but that was all we could muster up the energy for.

"I can't believe you're sixteen," Mom kept saying. "Sixteen years." And she looked at Madeline snoozing in her car seat, and you could tell she was thinking, sixteen years and now I have to start all over. By the time Madeline was Jack's age, it would be thirty-two straight years of being nothing but a mother. Almost two-thirds of her entire life.

Addy's plane left at eleven-thirty that morning, so it would have got in around three o'clock Montreal time. She phoned me at eight in the evening to tell me the news: Casey hadn't picked her up at the airport. She'd tried phoning home and there was no answer. She had waited for an hour, and then gave up and took the bus, and when she got back to their apartment, Casey wasn't there. She was gone, gone completely, gone for good. Addy made me promise not to tell Mom or anyone, not even Jack, at least not until she'd had some time to decide what she wanted to do.

She figured her mom must have been gone for at least a week, maybe more, because the coffee cup by the sink had a bloom of green mold floating in it the size of a mandarin orange. Casey had taken all her things, all her clothes and her suitcase, all her toiletries and makeup and everything, all she left behind was an envelope with five hundred bucks, a receipt for January's rent, and a note that said, "I'm sorry." That's all it said. It looked like she had started to write something else, but she'd scratched it out, going over it with the pen so many times that you couldn't read it at all, and the paper was almost torn. She even took her guitar. That was the part that pissed Addy off the most. She said, "Now I'm gonna have to buy my own, goddammit." I didn't even tell her that she should come and live with us. I guess I just felt too tired to try.

After I got off the phone with Addy I went straight to bed and I slept for something like fifteen hours straight. I didn't dream at all I slept so deep, and when I woke, I didn't even miss having Addy there like I usually do. I woke up thinking about whether I'd see Conrad that day, and maybe we would make our date for next weekend, and I felt happy and a little silly. Then I looked over at the clock, and I was startled. Mom had just let me keep sleeping even though it was the first day back at school, it was almost noon. I'd completely slept through morning classes.

Rose's picture was on the front page of the newspaper that morning. Two pictures actually, a big one of her body beneath the snowbank as they'd discovered it, looking so peaceful and composed, and a little inset of last year's school photo, with empty eyes and a forced fake smile. Apparently the caretaker from the community center had discovered her when he was shovelling out the Devil's Walk. At first glance he'd thought it was just an old boot sticking out of the snow, down there on the bank, and he almost walked away without looking any closer. But something told him to look again, to trudge through the snow and down the bank and take a closer look: "Just something," he was quoted as saying, "Like God or something whispering in my ear."

Jack saw the pictures and the paper first, and then when Mom and Davey saw it, they told him he could stay home from school for the day if he wanted to, but he said he wanted to go. But they decided to just let me sleep. So when I finally did wake up, pretty confused by the time on the clock and the bright sun streaming in my window, there was just Mom and the baby still home. I found them sitting in the living room waiting for me, waiting to tell me. Mom was holding Madeline at her breast and just kind of calmly silently crying.

ACKNOWLEDGEMENTS

It takes only one person to write a book, but it takes a whole village to put up with his crap while he's doing it. I want to give thanks to all my family, friends, and colleagues for putting up with mine. Except this one guy I know, he can go to hell.

I'd like to give particular thanks to the Manitoba Arts Council, for being all councilly and slipping me some money; to Kris Rothstein, for giving me invaluable feedback towards a final draft; and to all the good folk at Great Plains, especially Anita Daher, who has been both a smart, perceptive and sympathetic editor, and an energetic and generous advocate. Her enthusiasm for this book has been humbling and inspiring, so: Thank you.